Hey You, Sister Rose

EILEEN WALSH STRAUCH

Hey You, Sister Rose

Tambourine Books　New York

Library of Congress Cataloging in Publication Data

Strauch, Eileen Walsh
Hey you, Sister Rose/by Eileen Walsh Strauch.—1st ed. p. cm.
Summary: Arlene, a young girl growing up in Baltimore during the
early 1950s, has her worst nightmare come true when she gets the
dreaded Sister Rose for her sixth grade teacher.
[1. Nuns—Fiction.   2. Teachers—Fiction.   3. Catholic schools—
Fiction.   4. Schools—Fiction.   5. Baltimore (Md.)—Fiction.]   I. Title.
PZ7.S91227He   1993   [Fic]—dc20   92-12170   CIP   AC
ISBN 0-688-11829-1 (RTE)
1   3   5   7   9   10   8   6   4   2
First edition

For my parents, Regina and Andrew,
who never stopped believing in me,
even during those roller coaster
"Sister Rose" years

CONTENTS

CHAPTER 1

Sister Mary Rose

"ARLENE, STOP MOANING!" my sister whispered into the darkness.

I rolled over and glanced at the clock on the nightstand—a little past midnight.

"Why are you so worried about having Sister Rose anyway?" Janice asked. "She's strict, but nice. At least she's young and pretty. Some of the nuns at St. Anthony's School are as old as dirt. Anyway *I* never had any trouble with Sister Rose."

Jan never had trouble with any of the nuns because she was smart and cute and always did what she was supposed to. How could I tell her that it didn't matter if Sister Rose was young or old? The fact was, Sister Rose had it in for me—she *wanted* me to be in her class so she could get those hands with the long skinny fingers on me. And if she did, I'd never see 1952.

I'd relived the reason for Sister's wish umpteen times. It happened last Good Friday, when my best friend Nancy Lee and I were in church.

Everyone in my house had to go to church at least once on Good Friday. Since the Stations of the Cross were held in the afternoon and usually lasted only half an hour, Nancy and I decided to go then.

The Stations of the Cross are pictures or carvings hanging on the walls around the church. They each portray an occurrence leading up to Christ's crucifixion and death.

In front of each one, Father Fitzsimmons said a prayer, genuflected, said another prayer, then knelt for a minute.

Everything was fine until the third Station, when I noticed the cracking noise. I tried to ignore it by concentrating on the service, but I couldn't block out the sound.

Nancy Lee and I realized the source of the noise at precisely the same moment. We glanced at each other then burst out laughing. An old lady occupied the pew in front of us, and when she genuflected, her knees made a loud cracking sound.

Just when I thought I had the laughing under control, Father Fitzsimmons would say, "Let us kneel," and *cr-rack!* would go the knees.

Somehow Nancy managed to stifle her giggles, but with each pop I'd start all over again.

When the Stations finally ended, Nancy and I

clamped our hands over our mouths as if we were ready to puke and fled down the aisle toward the rear of the church.

We'd almost reached it when I saw Sister Mary Rose over by one of the confessionals. She cocked a finger, beckoning me to her.

Taking a deep breath, I inched in her direction. As soon as I got close she grabbed my arm and propelled me out the side door.

"Aren't you Janice Warren's sister?" she asked, her deep blue eyes boring into me.

I was so scared, all I could do was nod and gawk at my feet as if they'd each grown an extra toe.

"You should be ashamed of yourself," she breathed, "acting like that in church on one of the holiest days of the year." With an exasperated sigh she jerked my chin skyward. "Look at me when I'm speaking to you, young lady. Why did you come to church if you weren't going to behave properly?"

I shrugged, noticing how fiery red her face had become and wondering how Nancy Lee had managed to slip out the other side door without Sister noticing. After all, she'd been laughing too.

"What do you think your parents or Sister Teresa would say? You *are* in Sister Teresa's class. Aren't you?"

I nodded again.

"Don't rattle your brains at me, child," she cried. "Speak when you're spoken to."

"Yes, Sister," I mumbled through chattering teeth. "I'm sorry, Sister."

She released the tourniquet grip on my arm. "Well, you should be. Your older brother, Edward, was one of my students, too, a while back. He wasn't as smart as Janice, but he was always respectful. I'm going to have to keep an eye on you, Miss Warren."

Right now she had *two* eyes on me, and it felt as if they were scalding my brain.

"You would probably benefit from being in my class next year. *I'd* keep you in line." She continued glaring for what seemed an eternity before she said, "And you'd better perform some act of sacrifice in repentance for your conduct today."

"Yes, Sister. I will, Sister." She could've told me to jump off the roof and I would've said yes— anything to get away from those piercing blue orbs.

"All right, you can go. But remember, *I'll be watching you!*"

For a long time after that day, I'd wake up in the middle of the night thinking I'd heard those words— seen those eyes. And as the second week in September and a new school year drew close, I imagined them more and more.

"Sometimes Sister Agatha teaches sixth grade." Jan's voice pulled me from my half-dream. "Maybe you'll get her. Everybody knows she's great. Now shut up and go to sleep!"

I told myself that I would get Sister Agatha, but like a record with the needle stuck, Sister Rose's warning played itself over and over in my head until I fell asleep.

When I awoke the next morning, Janice, already up and dressed, was standing in front of her bureau taking kid curlers out of her hair. As long as I could remember, Jan had been using kid curlers. They reminded me of flat cigars. Her hair always looked good, but she was forever griping because I had gotten the silky blond hair. I didn't care what color my hair was. But if it bugged Jan, that made me happy.

"I hate uniforms," Jan grumbled. "You'd think they could come up with something prettier than this brown jumper. It's exactly the same color as Daddy's coffee after he puts cream in it. Ugh!"

"How do you think the nuns feel?" I asked, yawning. "They have to wear black and white all the time."

Ignoring me, she gathered the material at the waistline and stuck out her chest. "If it just weren't so darn baggy. Just think, Arlene, this time next year I'll be starting high school and I won't have to wear this horrible thing anymore."

I yawned again and sat on the side of the bed. "Yeah, but you'll still be wearing some kind of uniform."

"At least it won't be this one!" She paused, then asked, "Do you ever think about living somewhere more exciting?"

"What's wrong with Baltimore? I like Baltimore!"

"Oh, you're such a baby!" she said, stomping

from the room. But before she slammed the door, she called back over her shoulder, "I hope you *do* get Sister Rose. She'll skin you alive!"

All Janice's stupid talk about uniforms and leaving Baltimore had made me forget about Sister Rose. Suddenly I felt as if I'd swallowed a live fish, scales and all. Maybe I could skip school today—tell Mama I was sick. It wasn't really a lie. I was tempted to crawl back under the covers, but before I had a chance she came to the door.

"You better hurry up or you won't have time to eat."

I groaned, stood up, and headed for the bathroom.

After dressing I went into the dining room, where our family spent most of its time. My house had a small living room that Mama called the front room, a kitchen you couldn't eat in, and two bedrooms, all on the first floor. Upstairs, Daddy had finished off the attic into two rooms where my brothers slept.

We always seemed to congregate around our dining room table. The only members of the family who weren't there this morning were my dad, who ran his own hardware-lumber business and went to work before any of us younger kids got up, and my brother Ed, a senior at Loyola High School. He had to take two buses to get there so he left real early too.

Mikey, playing with the bowl of cornflakes in front of him, was starting second grade today. He could be a brat, but right now he looked kind of cute in his long brown pants, white shirt, and brown tie.

"It'll just be you and me today," Mama said to three-year-old Danny. She didn't seem especially unhappy with that prospect.

A stack of toast, three jars of cereal, and a bottle of milk occupied the middle of the oilcloth-covered table. Mama always poured new boxes of cereal into large jars to keep it fresh. One time I heard Daddy say he didn't know why she bothered because the food in this house never seemed to last long enough to get stale.

I was hungry, but was sure if I ate something, I'd be sick. It was hours till lunch so I grabbed a piece of toast.

Nancy Lee's red hair glowed in the morning sunshine as she waited for me on the front steps.

Jan, Mike, and I waved good-bye to Mama and Danny, then we all trooped toward school.

Nancy and I knew we were in room 102 together. We just didn't know which nun would be teaching us. Jan had had Sister Rose in seventh grade. Maybe she'd be seventh-grade teacher this year. But sometimes the nuns switched classrooms during the summer. I'm convinced they did it just to keep us guessing and to make us suffer.

The four of us walked about a block and a half up Greenhill Avenue toward school. As soon as we cut through the wooded vacant lot that led to the parking lot, we heard the bedlam.

There had always been designated areas on the

school grounds for each grade to stand. At first bell Nancy Lee and I ran to the sixth-grade spot. Jan grabbed Mike's hand and deposited him with the other second-graders before taking her place with the eighth grade.

Our principal, Sister Alma Regina, stood on the school steps surveying the sea of students.

Glancing around, I noticed several sixth-graders I didn't recognize, including a girl with stringy brown hair and rumpled uniform, and a good-looking boy big enough to be in high school. He seemed vaguely familiar.

Some of the nuns were helping to keep order, but Sister Rose wasn't among them.

As soon as the second bell sounded, that mob of unruly, screaming kids formed eight silent, orderly lines, and when the third bell rang, we marched up the steps and into the large brick building.

As we passed, Sister Alma said, "Children, please go quickly and quietly to your assigned rooms. The hall monitors will assist anyone who needs help."

Since I still didn't see Sister Rose, I said a quick prayer that she'd been transferred—to Alaska!

We filed into a teacherless room 102. Each desk had a name on it. As I searched and found mine, I saw that someone named Eunice Montgomery had the seat next to me.

As soon as I slid into my seat Annette Carlson, the prissiest girl in the class and the biggest drag imaginable, whispered sarcastically, "Oh, goody,

I'm sitting near my *favorite* person. That reminds me, Arlene, want to know how to lose ten pounds of ugly fat?" She snickered. "Just cut off your head!" Her perfect blond curls bounced as she chuckled to herself.

"Hardeeharhar," I answered not too softly. "That joke's as old as—as—Sister Rose is mean." I turned to sit down, and in that instant all my most horrible nightmares came true.

Like the warden of Sing Sing prison, Sister Mary Rose, a deep scowl creasing her face and arms folded across her chest, stood behind her desk. I wasn't sure if she'd heard what I'd said, but I *was* sure I didn't like the satisfied gleam in those eyes as they stared directly at me.

CHAPTER 2

Understanding Each Other

BEFORE SISTER ROSE could say anything another bell sounded and we all stood up for prayers. I was sure that if that bell hadn't rung, she would've bawled me out. I don't know if it was the prayers or what, but after the amens Sister was like a different person.

Lifting her chin, she announced, "I am Sister Mary Rose."

The way she said it, you would've thought she was telling us she was Saint Joan of Arc.

She wrote her name on the board, turned, and said, "We have several new people this year. So why don't we have everyone introduce themselves?" She pointed to Maria Lusco in the first row. "You start and we'll go around the room."

As each kid stood up, Sister told something about them. When Eunice Montgomery, the girl with the wrinkled uniform, rose, Sister said, "Eunice's family moved from South Carolina in the middle of April."

The whole time Sister was talking about her, Eunice stared at her feet, and she was shaking like she'd caught a sudden chill. I wondered why Eunice hadn't come to school in April. Had she gone to public school or just played hooky for two months?

"Obviously she doesn't know what soap is," Annette whispered to her sidekick, Connie Rapchinski.

For once I had to agree with Annette. Eunice's skin was the color of old Silly Putty. She didn't smell too great either.

Suddenly Eunice stood up straight and held her head high. She must have heard the nasty crack.

I chuckled to myself when I noticed Annette's face. It surprised her that her lousy remark hadn't gotten to Eunice. Hooray for Eunice, I thought.

But then I started to worry, imagining what Sister would say when she introduced me—"Arlene Warren is the most disrespectful student in the whole school!"

My heart knocked against my rib cage while I waited, but when I stood up, all Sister said was, "Arlene's family has been in our parish for many years. Her brother and sister were both students of mine." I sat down with a huge sigh of relief.

When Sister reached the tall boy I'd noticed earlier, he acted as if he was having trouble getting up from his desk. His long legs had been crossed, and when he finally stood he was facing the back of the room.

"Lee Hunt," he announced to the rear cloakroom in a booming voice.

Everybody laughed.

Sister banged her desk. "Turn around, Lee."

Lee spun around on one foot, slamming into his desk.

Now I knew why he'd looked familiar. Janice had talked about some guy named Lee who'd failed several times. That was why he was so big. He was her age, maybe older. She'd described him as dumb but funny. I just thought he was obnoxious.

"Sit down, Mr. Hunt, so we can finish our introductions."

When all forty names had been called Sister said, "Before we begin our work I'd like to explain a few things about my class. I will not put up with shirkers or clowns." Her no-nonsense gaze rested on Lee. "And I do not tolerate any shenanigans. Do I make myself perfectly clear?"

Although I lowered my eyelids I was certain that she was remembering Good Friday and that her last remark was meant for me.

Finally she began to teach by writing a long division problem on the board, and I just knew when she chose someone to do it I would be that someone. I was right.

I hated arithmetic and it hated me. If I'd been

home I could've figured out the answer eventually, but standing up in front of everyone and having a time limit, I was lost.

Since it was obvious I didn't know what I was doing, Sister asked if anyone would like to take over. Old snot-nosed Annette stuck her hand in the air. Sister called her and, of course, she solved the problem as fast as if she were adding two plus two.

Wearing a smirk, Annette sauntered back to her seat. As she passed me, she whispered, "Simple, unless you're stupid."

I was tempted to trip her, but I knew that wouldn't make such a good first-day impression, especially since Sister already had it in for me.

After arithmetic Sister moved on to geography, another of my un-favorite subjects. I couldn't understand why I had to know about Brazil when I lived in the United States.

So as Sister's voice droned on about Brazil's population, temperatures, and agriculture, my mind wandered. I thought about lunch. We'd had homemade chicken-noodle soup for supper the night before. I loved Mama's chicken soup. I hoped there'd be some left for lunch.

Then somewhere in the midst of my musings, I vaguely heard my name and glanced up.

Like an impatient woodpecker, Sister rapidly tapped the map of Brazil with a wooden pointer. Her eyes on me were alight with hope. "Do you know the answer, Arlene?"

Slowly I pushed to my feet. Everyone was staring. I even detected a few snickers. "I'm sorry, Sister, could you repeat the question?"

Sister *whacked* the palm of her hand with the pointer, her face exploding with color. She glowered in icy silence. I'd heard about some nuns smacking kids' knuckles with rulers. Was Sister Rose one of the smackers?

I didn't have a chance to find out, thank goodness, because—*swish, swish*—like someone brandishing a sword, Sister suddenly aimed the stick at none other than Annette.

I was still recovering from my humiliation when Sister asked us to take out our English textbooks. She began reviewing grammar by giving us several questions. I knew the answers but didn't raise my hand just in case I might be wrong.

Next she put a sentence on the board with no punctuation and several grammatical errors. She requested a volunteer to correct it.

I was sure I could do it. But suppose I did it wrong? While I was debating about whether or not to raise my hand, Sister called on Jane Kane, who went to the board and fixed the sentence accurately, exactly the way I would have done it.

Right before the lunch bell Sister announced, "On Friday, we are going to have a spelling bee using the word lists from fourth and fifth grades. I want to see how much you retained over the summer. After lunch I'll hand out the lists. There are a total of three hundred words, so I suggest you start studying today."

I grinned. Spelling was one thing I was good at. I was always winning spelling bees and had several certificates and at least one plaque to prove it.

I'd show Sister Mary Rose that I wasn't a complete dope. My grin broadened when I recalled what a terrible speller Annette was!

The lunch bell rang and Sister told the walkers they could leave. Walkers were the students who lived close enough to go home for lunch. I headed for the door.

"Arlene Warren," Sister said, "please stay a moment."

My heart pounded in my chest while I watched the walkers leave and the rest of the class head to the lunchroom. After they'd gone, Sister said, "Miss Warren, maybe you didn't think I remembered your little incident in church last Good Friday." Those blue eyes challenged me. "Well, I want you to know I remember it vividly." As she fiddled with the rosary beads hanging from her belt, little red spots began to form on her cheeks. They looked like Mama's rouge before she smooths it out.

"I had hoped we understood each other this morning when I gave my little talk," she continued in that tight-lipped manner I'd already recognized as irritation. "But it's obvious by your attitude that you didn't understand. Not paying attention is as bad as carrying on in class, and I will not tolerate either." Her eyes flashed. "Now do we understand each other?"

"Yes, Sister," I muttered.

"I didn't hear you," she cried.

I raised my head and glared straight into those blazing peepers. "Yes, Sister, I understand *you*." I swallowed hard and added softly, "But I doubt if you understand *me*!"

I didn't hang around long enough to find out if Sister had realized what I'd said—I ran out of there as fast as Mikey runs when he hears the word *bath*.

This was only the first day of school. How was I ever going to make it to the last?

CHAPTER 3

So-prah-no

As I FLED toward home I knew I was in big trouble. Why was I always making things worse? If I'd just kept my mouth shut . . .

Mama, Jan, Mike, and Danny were already eating lunch as I entered the house.

Mama frowned. "What took you so long?"

I shrugged.

Before I sat down, Jan asked, "Well, did you?"

"Did I what?"

"Get Sister Rose."

I nodded.

"So? How do you like her?" She jutted her chin. "I got Sister Alma!"

Jan always lucked out. Besides being the principal and a great teacher, Sister Alma was super nice.

I tried to ignore Jan's question by stirring my soup. It smelled delicious, but I'd lost my appetite. Even Mama's chicken-noodle soup couldn't bring it back today. I ate a few spoonsful then asked to be excused.

Jan smirked. "Don't tell me you're in trouble with Sister already!"

"Can't a person not be hungry?" I shouted, jumping up and running into the yard. I had to think! My thinking place was our apple tree.

The huge tree grew right outside of Jan's and my bedroom. In spring each breeze stirred up a confetti shower of blossom petals before carrying the sweet fragrance inside.

Being careful not to tear my uniform, I climbed up to my seat. Actually it was where two gnarled branches formed a *U*. The seat used to fit me perfectly, but lately it felt a little snug.

I don't ever remember grass growing around the tree, I guess because my little brothers were always playing underneath with their toy cars and trucks. They carved roads, hollowed out tunnels, and constructed parking lots. They'd dug so deep that most of the roots were exposed now. The roots reminded me of hundreds of snakes crawling all over each other.

Daddy kept saying he was going to bring in a load of topsoil to cover them up. "You boys are going to kill that tree," he'd yell. But it bloomed year after year and, year after year, provided apples. I'd hear them dropping like bombs in the middle of the night.

The sound never frightened me. In a way, it was reassuring.

Shifting in my seat, I gazed at the woods across the street. The trees spread their leaves across an endless blue sky.

Out of the corner of my eye, I saw the church spire. Though I didn't want to, it forced me to think of Sister Rose and my problem.

What would she do when I returned? I *had* been disrespectful. Would I have to tell that in confession? More than anything, I wished that I didn't have to go back to school. I'd say I was sick. But even if Mama let me stay home this afternoon—and I knew she wouldn't—I couldn't play hooky forever.

Perched about level with the attic, I could see down into my bedroom. Jan came in, squeezed a pimple, combed her hair, then sauntered out.

Now Mama was in there. By the way she was acting I knew she was searching for me. She left but returned a few minutes later. "Arlene," she called out the window, "are you in that tree again?"

"Yes, Mama."

"You have exactly seven minutes until the bell rings. Get in here—and be careful! If you rip that uniform . . ." She paused. "Well, if you do, I'm going to say something!"

Mama never, ever, said a bad word; she was always just *going* to.

Hopping down from the tree, I brushed off the back of my dress and rushed into the house. I washed my hands at the kitchen sink, grabbed a piece of bread from the plate just as Mama was about to put it into its wrapper, and dashed out the front door.

If I thought I was in trouble before, all I needed was to be late!

I sped up Greenhill Avenue, trying to chew the wad of soft, doughy bread I'd stuffed into my mouth. I had almost reached the vacant lot behind school when the bell rang. My class was already filing into the building. I don't think Sister noticed me slip into line.

When I sat at my desk my heart was fluttering like the wings of a hummingbird. I couldn't catch my breath. For a moment I thought I might faint. I'd fainted in church once and, boy, did people make a fuss over me!

I decided that if I didn't look directly at Sister, maybe she'd forget that I'd sassed her. But she had to think I was paying attention. So I spent the afternoon staring at the cross hanging around her neck. Once Sister called on me and, thank goodness, I knew the answer.

Right before dismissal Sister Alma's voice came over the public address system. "Any boy or girl in the sixth, seventh, or eighth grade who would like to join the children's choir is asked to come to the church immediately after school. This is for new members only."

For as long as I could remember I'd wanted to be in the choir. My family was musical. Mama played the piano, Daddy had a beautiful tenor voice and belonged to St. Anthony's adult choir, and Jan had been in the children's choir since sixth grade.

I held my breath when the bell rang, hoping Sister Rose wouldn't tell me to stay.

"The walkers may go now," she said.

Those hummingbird wings beat again as I headed toward the door. I kept my eyes riveted ahead long after I'd made it into the hallway.

Once outside, though, I bounded over to the church as if Sister Rose were chasing me with a club. I heard whispers as I scrambled up the winding narrow steps leading to the loft. I don't know how she did it, but Annette was already there talking to a girl from seventh grade. She made a face at me. "Why do you always have to do everything *I* do?"

Before I had a chance to answer, several other kids emerged, followed by a panting Sister Alma, whose face was blotchy and sweaty. She always looked so uncomfortable in her habit. Daddy called her pleasingly plump. I wondered how she managed to stay so pleasant when the starched white piece framing her face appeared to be cutting into her flesh. I almost expected to see blood when she turned her head.

She scanned the loft, counting—fifteen girls and five boys. "Thank you for coming, children. I had hoped to interest a few more boys this time, but . . ." Sitting at the organ, she began to play "Holy God, We Praise Thy Name." "You're all familiar with that. Aren't you?"

"Yes, Sister," we chorused.

"Okay." She glanced at me. "Arlene, please turn to page sixty-seven in the hymnal."

I did as requested, amazed at how she knew everyone's name. I figured that was why she'd been chosen principal.

"What I'd like to do is have each of you sing a few lines from 'Holy God.' "

"Alone?" I gasped.

She chuckled. "Don't be nervous. This is only to determine which part you'll sing." She smiled again. "Who would like to be first?"

Silence.

"Well, Arlene, since you're holding the book, why don't you start. I'll play it through again."

The hummingbirds were back, but this time they occupied my stomach. Stepping close to the organ, I gazed at the altar below, votive lights twinkling in the dimness. I opened my mouth and started to vocalize *holy*. Nothing came out but *ho* and a whoosh of air. I heard giggles. Sister ignored them, gave me a reassuring nod, and began the music once more. I took a deep breath and sang as clear and as on key as I possibly could.

Sister stopped playing. "Thank you, Arlene, that was very nice. You sound like a soprano to me."

I'd made it! I was a soprano. I liked the way the word rolled off my tongue. *So-prah-no!* For a moment I imagined myself on the stage of the Metropolitan Opera with an announcer saying, "Ladies and gentlemen, it is my great pleasure to present the totally fabulous *so-prah-no*, Miss Arlene Warren."

"Didn't you hear me, Arlene?" Sister Alma's voice interrupted my daydream. "I said you may sit down now."

I blushed and quickly took a seat. *So-prah-no*, I thought again, remembering that Jan sang soprano too. She'd have a fit if I had to stand beside her. I grinned.

Annette was up next. When she sang, a lot of the kids snickered. I even noticed Sister biting her twitching lips. And no wonder! Annette sang everything in a monotone, except that when a note was supposed to go up she got louder. If it went down, she became softer. Obviously spelling wasn't the only thing Annette was lousy at.

When Annette had completed her audition, Sister frowned slightly, though I don't think she was aware of the frown. She said, "Annette, you have one of those in-between voices. You'll have to let me think about where to put you."

I could've suggested where to put her!

Annette beamed as if she'd been told she had a voice like a canary.

"Now, children," Sister said when everyone had finished, "I want you to think seriously before you commit yourselves to the choir. Who can tell me what a commitment is?"

My hand shot up.

"Yes, Arlene?"

"It's like a promise or . . ."

"Precisely. You are promising to come to practice once a week. Practice is on Tuesday mornings before school—at eight A.M. And the choir sings every Sunday at the nine o'clock children's Mass. This is what you are committing yourselves to if you join. So before you make a decision, please think about it. Then if you still want to be a member, come next Tuesday morning. Practice begins then."

She dismissed us and, as I trotted toward home, I relived her compliment. "Very nice, Arlene," she had told me. She'd only said nice, okay, or fine to the other kids. But to me, it was very nice!

I smiled. With choir and Sister Alma to look forward to each week, maybe I'd somehow make it through Sister Rose's sixth grade.

CHAPTER 4

Challenges

"I MADE IT!" I shrieked, slamming through the front door. "I'm in the choir. Sister said I have a very nice *so-prah-no* voice and—"

Mama and Aunt Gussie came out of the kitchen. Aunt Gussie, Mama's oldest sister, was like my grandmother, since she'd practically raised Mom after their mother died. Aunt Gussie lived with Aunt Agnes, another unmarried sister, who went out to work while Aunt Gussie stayed home and kept house.

"What are you yelling about?" Mama asked.

I ran over and hugged them both. "I'm going to be in the children's choir. Sister said I have a very nice voice."

Aunt Gussie chuckled. "Well, I should think so. You belong to a musical family."

"Where's Jan?" I asked.

"She's over at Margie's."

"Darn, I wanted to tell her. Oh, well, she'll find out soon enough."

I scurried into the bedroom and changed my clothes. While I waited for Jan to get home, I thought about how to tell her I was in the choir. She'd have a cow when she found out I was singing soprano.

But even after she came home I decided to hold off with my announcement until the whole family was seated for dinner. Then I casually remarked, "Guess what, Daddy? I made the choir today!"

He smiled. "Good for you. I think you'll enjoy—"

"Big deal," cried Jan. "Sister lets everybody in, even people like you who can't carry a tune in a bucket." Then she looked worried. "What part are you singing?"

I ignored her dig by granting her one of my most charming smiles. "*So-prah-no*," I said with a syrupy voice. "And for your information, Sister Alma said I have an excellent voice." I figured it wouldn't hurt to exaggerate a little.

She scowled. "Don't think you're going to stand next to me. And you won't think it's so great when you have to be up at six-thirty every Tuesday morning to get to practice by eight. You hate getting up!"

"Why would I have to get up at six-thirty? It doesn't take me as long as you to get ready."

"You don't think *I'm* getting up first, do you?"

"Girls," Dad said, "you can work that out later. But Janice, why do you care if Arlene's in the choir? Singing is good for the soul."

"I can sing," Danny said, demonstrating with, "A, B, C, D, E, F, G—H, I, J, K, Al and Manny pee."

We all burst out laughing.

But Mama and Aunt Gussie frowned. "Danny, where did you learn that?"

He shrugged, glancing at Mikey.

Mike stared at his plate a few seconds, then said, "I know a Christmas song. 'Hark the *harelip* angels sing. *Gwowy* . . .' "

We laughed again, but Mama said, "Michael, that's not very nice."

"Want to hear another song?" Danny asked.

"No, I think we've had enough singing," Daddy said, and changed the subject. "Your mother tells me you have a spelling bee coming up, Arlene. When is it?"

"Friday."

"Well, make sure you study."

"I will, but I need somebody to call out the words for me."

"I'll help you Thursday night," Daddy said. "That way everything will be fresh in your mind."

I sure would be glad when the spelling bee was over. Besides, after Friday I'd only have three more days until choir started. But I had to get through the spelling bee first, and I had to do well. If I actually won, then maybe Sister wouldn't hate me or think I was stupid. Perhaps she'd even forget that I'd sassed her.

I spent at least an hour on my spelling that night after I did my other homework, and I stayed out of trouble for the next couple of days.

Thursday morning Annette and Connie challenged Nancy Lee and me to a double dutch contest.

"We all know that *I* can jump longer than either of you," Annette said.

"Who says?" I sneered.

"Wasn't I double dutch champion last year?"

"That was last year," Nancy Lee pointed out in her calm, even manner. "But to determine the current double dutch champ," she continued like a radio sportscaster, "you'll have to defend your title."

We made plans to have the contest after lunch. At home I gulped down my food and then barreled back up to the school ground with my jump rope. The blustery September wind stung my cheeks. If it hadn't been for that wind, I might not have noticed Eunice Montgomery hunched over, sitting on a rainspout behind school, in an *L*-shaped corner of the building. Her red sweater flapped around her like a warning flag. I'd noticed the sweater this morning because it hung way below her knees and was big enough to fit my brother Ed.

I didn't want to stop and talk. If I did, I might not have time for the contest. I'd never spoken to Eunice except in class. Nobody talked to her. I knew it was because of her appearance. Some of the kids made fun of her, especially Annette, who said she had cooties. She also said she'd heard that Eunice's house was roach heaven.

Eunice hadn't seen me because she had her hands over her face. I quickened my pace and had almost rounded the bend toward the playground when I glanced back. I was immediately sorry I'd done that because it made me wonder if she might be sick. Was she crying? I couldn't stand to see someone cry. I headed back.

"Eunice," I asked as I got closer, "are you all right?"

She didn't move.

"Eunice?"

She raised her head. Her bleary eyes stared at me as if she didn't know who I was. I couldn't tell if she'd been crying or sleeping. Eunice always seemed tired.

"You okay?"

She made a noise that sounded like a laugh, but it was definitely *not* a laugh.

"Maybe you should go in and get your jacket," I suggested because I couldn't think of anything else to say. Then I remembered that I hadn't seen her wearing a jacket this morning. "It's much colder today than yesterday, isn't it?"

She grabbed a fistful of sweater where several buttons were missing. "I'm okay," she mumbled, lowering her head again.

Then I really didn't know what to do. Mama and Aunt Gussie would've told me to ask her to jump rope with us. But if I did that, Annette and Connie would never let me hear the end of it. I knew Nancy Lee wouldn't care but, truth was, I didn't want everybody saying I was Eunice's friend. I sort of felt sorry for her. But suppose Annette was right and Eunice did have cooties?

I stood there expecting her to say or do something. When she didn't, I decided she wanted to be alone and ran around to the playground.

"Where have you been?" demanded Annette. "You must've had a really big lunch. We've been waiting forever!"

"I was detained," I said, using one of our spelling words.

Annette grabbed the jump rope, handed two ends to me and the looped part to Nancy Lee. "I'm first," she said.

I threw the rope back at Annette. "Oh, no, you're not. It's my rope. I'm first."

"Who cares? It's probably better if you go first anyway because we don't have much time and you won't last long. You're lousy at double dutch."

"Ha! We'll just see."

Annette and Connie started turning the ropes.

I glanced at Nancy Lee. "Count for me, okay?"

She nodded.

Before I could jump in, Lee Hunt appeared out of nowhere and leapt into the middle of the ropes, saying in a high-pitched voice, "Johnny and Annette sitting in a tree, K-I-S-S-I-N-G . . ."

Annette snatched the rope away. "Get out of here, Lee Hunt, or I'm telling Sister."

"I'm telling Sister," Lee mimicked.

Nancy and I laughed. Lee vanished as fast as he came.

Annette and Connie turned the ropes again.

I rocked back and forth waiting for the perfect moment to jump in. Just as I made my move, I saw Eunice coming around the side of the building and, in the split second before I skipped into the middle of the whirling ropes, our eyes met.

I heard the slap, slap, slap of the rope hitting the pavement, Nancy Lee saying, "Ten, eleven, twelve . . ." I saw blurry images of Annette and Connie anxiously waiting for me to miss. But I sensed rather than saw Eunice's sad, pale face watching me. Then I remembered something Aunt Gussie told Mama once. "Take Ida Trent, for instance. I believe that poor soul would be lonely in a crowd." I didn't know who Ida Trent was, and I could never figure out what Aunt Gussie had meant until now.

The school ground is filled with kids, I thought, but poor Eunice . . . Before I had a chance to finish my thought, my feet became tangled in the ropes.

"Ha, told you, Arlene," Annette cried with glee. "You stink!"

CHAPTER 5

Hey You

I CONVINCED MYSELF that Eunice caused my double dutch goof-up. Not that it was her fault—I just thought that I missed because I hadn't asked her to play.

Now, worried about the same thing happening with the spelling bee, I tried to be nicer to Eunice. If I had to hand her a paper, I'd smile. Once Eunice couldn't seem to find her pen, so I asked if she wanted to borrow one. She just said, "I've got it here somewhere." Funny thing was, she didn't act any differently than she had all along.

As I headed home that afternoon, I wondered if things really did work that way. If you weren't nice to someone, would something bad happen because of it?

Maybe I'd ask Jan. When I entered our bedroom, she lay sprawled across her bed like a polka-dotted rag doll with dabs of Noxema all over her face.

As always she had the radio blaring.

"Jan," Mama called from the kitchen, "turn that radio down!"

Begrudgingly she reached over and turned the knob. "I'm waiting for them to play 'Tennessee Waltz,'" she said, "and I don't want to miss it."

"You couldn't miss it if you were in the bathroom with the water running."

Even though Jan made a face at me, she laughed.

Slipping out of my uniform, I threw it across the bed, then stepped into a pair of dungarees and an old shirt of Ed's.

Jan seemed to be in a good mood so I asked, "Do you think that if a person does something not so nice, then that person will be repaid by something bad happening to them?"

She frowned, making the dried Noxema cream flake like dandruff. "Huh?"

"I mean—"

She didn't let me finish. "What'd you do now?"

"I didn't do anything. I was just asking." I paused, deciding how to rephrase the question. "Suppose you know you should be nice to somebody but, for some reason, you don't want to. So you just ignore the person. Then something bad happens to you."

Jan rose from the bed. "What bad thing happened to you and who were you ignoring?"

"I told you, I'm not talking about me! I was just wondering why bad things happen to some people and not to others."

She sat down at her dresser and stared back at me from the mirror. "For gosh sakes, if I knew that, I'd be God!"

Sorry that I'd brought up the subject, I changed it abruptly by asking, "Guess who's in my class? Lee Hunt. Boy, is he obnoxious! Why does he act like that?"

Jan leaned closer to the mirror. "Who knows? He'll probably be thirty before he gets out of St. Anthony's. He drives the nuns crazy."

"Yeah, he's been acting up already."

Jan shook her head. "You'd think he'd hate being kept back. He is kind of funny, though. He should probably go into show business." She turned toward me. "Speaking of show business, Margie's family bought a television. She said I could come over Saturday night and watch it with her." Jan sighed. "It'll probably be years before we get one."

"Daddy said we can't afford it."

"We're always the last people to get something new. I hate being poor!" She snatched up the magazine she'd been reading and strode from the room.

Were we poor? I'd never really thought about it before. And I didn't want to think about it now. Jan hadn't solved my problem about whether I'd made the bad stuff happen, so I knew I'd better be well prepared for the spelling bee.

I studied until Mama said supper was ready. As

soon as the table was cleared afterward, Daddy began quizzing me. We'd gotten through most of the word list before he gave me *restaurant* to spell.

"R-e-s-t-u-a—"

"No, try again."

"I can never remember how to spell that stupid word," I moaned, slumping into my chair. "Can't I stop now?"

"Just as soon as you get *restaurant* right."

I sounded out the word in my mind and said, "R-e-s-t-a . . ." I was stuck. I started over. "R-e-s-t-a . . ." I glanced at Dad. "Is that right so far?"

He nodded.

Why was it I could spell every other word on the list but I couldn't spell *restaurant*? Taking a long gulp of air, I said quickly, "R-e-s-t-a-r-a-n-t."

"A-U, A-U," shouted Dad, "not U-A and not just A. It's A-U! Why can't you get that into your head?"

"I don't know," I cried. We'd been working for hours, and I was starting to see letters floating in the air.

Mom rushed into the dining room. "Andy! Yelling at her isn't going to help. I think you've both had enough. It's time for her to go to bed anyway."

"Not until she spells this word right." He snapped his fingers. "I've got it! Just think of *hey you*."

I frowned. "Hey, you?"

"A-U—hey, you. Get it?"

"Oh, yeah, I see." I giggled and recited, "R-e-s-t-*hey-you*-r-a-n-t!" We all laughed.

———

Daddy handed me the list. "You'll be fine. Go to bed and just do your best tomorrow."

As Nancy Lee and I walked to school the next morning, I tried not to think about the spelling bee. I considered Dad's advice: "With two hundred and ninety-nine other words, there isn't much chance you'll get *restaurant* to spell anyway. If you do, just remember—*hey you*."

I hoped the bee would take place after morning announcements, but the blackboard gave the story in big, bold letters—SPELLING BEE AFTER LUNCH!

My stomach flip-flopped all through geography and arithmetic. Finally the lunch bell rang and I ran home as fast as I could.

At home, in between bites of my peanut butter and jelly sandwich, Mom called out words and I spelled them.

"*Restaurant*," Mom said.

I confidently pronounced each letter. "R-e-s-t-a-u-r-a-n-t!"

"Perfect!" She kissed me, wished me good luck, and I sang, "Hey you, A-U, hey you, A-U," all the way back to school.

I couldn't believe it, though, when Sister told us to take out our history books after class began again.

She's doing this on purpose, I thought. She knows I'm nervous and wants me to suffer.

But somehow I got through the history lesson, and then in that crystal-clear tone of hers, Sister said, "Please clean off your desks. We will now have the spelling bee." She looked directly at me.

"This will be an indication of who studied and who didn't."

I slid down in my seat. But why was I doing that? I was more than prepared.

Go ahead, I dared her silently, give me any word you've got.

"First of all," Sister said, "I'd like you all to move to the perimeter of the room. You may stand in any order you please, but do it quickly and quietly."

Nancy Lee signaled for me to get next to her, but I didn't want to. She was a good speller. If I was beside someone not so good, I'd probably have a better chance. I was looking for Annette when Sister said, "Arlene, there's room next to John Nardini."

Sighing, I walked to the side of the room, and Sister began the rules. "We will start with Maria Lusco and go around the room. If the student ahead of you spells his or her word incorrectly, then you must spell that word to stay in the competition. Very well, then . . ." She pushed up the sleeves of the sweater (or whatever it was) she wore under her habit, smoothed back her veil as if it were long hair, and said, "Maria, please spell *reference*."

I counted twelve kids ahead of me, and my heart beat faster with each name.

Carole got *moistening* to spell. Easy, I mumbled, but Carole left out the *t*. Sister gave her an evil look and told her to sit down. She called on Allan, who spelled it correctly.

I kept hoping Sister would give someone *restaurant* to spell. Get it over with, I thought.

I zipped each new word off in my head without the slightest hesitation.

Only three kids ahead of me. *Hey you*, A-U, I told myself. Both Mary and Eunice got easy words.

My heart was really racing now—John Nardini's turn. I was next!

"*Resource*." Sister pronounced the word distinctly.

Oh, please miss it, I whispered. Miss it and I'll spell it and Sister will smile.

John didn't miss it. He ticked off each letter as if he were spelling *dog* or *cat*.

Sister fixed her gaze on me. "Arlene, your word is"—I held my breath—"*restaurant*."

No! my mind screamed, she couldn't have said that. I stood there, frozen.

"Arlene, it's your turn." Sister's voice rose. "Spell *restaurant*."

Aware of forty pairs of eyes watching, I swallowed. My sandpaper tongue felt glued to the roof of my mouth. "Could you please repeat the word, Sister?" I croaked.

Folding her arms, she tucked her hands into the flowing sleeves of her habit and glowered at me. How well I knew that stance! "*Restaurant*—the word is *restaurant*!" The sound bounced off the walls.

My heart pounded so fast, I heard the rushing in my ears. I tried to recall what Dad had told me and mumbled, "Hey, you."

"Please speak up, Arlene!"

"R-e-s-t . . ." I hesitated, straining to picture the word in my head.

"Yes, go on."

"A-u-r . . ." My mind went blank. I paused once more, and far away in my brain a tiny voice repeated, *hey you–hey you.* So I continued with "a-u-n-t."

Snickering came from the back of the classroom as Sister said in a disgusted tone, "Oh, sit down, Arlene."

Annette, who was on the other side of me, also misspelled *restaurant*, but Sister's eyes, cold as blue stones, never left my face.

I don't know how I managed to sit through the rest of the bee without crying. As soon as the bell rang I raced out like a squirrel with its tail on fire. I tore up my front steps and slammed through the door. Mama came out of the kitchen, drying her hands. "How—"

"I hate spelling, I hate Sister Rose, and I hate *restaurants*," I sobbed before stomping into my room and hurling myself across the bed.

I stayed that way until Jan started pounding on the door. "Open up, you little twerp. You have no right locking me out."

"A person can't even be miserable in private in this house," I fumed as I unlocked the door.

"Mama said supper's almost ready," Jan announced, staying only long enough to comb her hair.

"I'm not hungry."

"Well, that's a first! You must be upset. I don't know why you're making such a big deal about a spelling bee."

You wouldn't, I thought, because all the nuns love you and you get good grades in everything. English is my best subject, and now I'll probably get a big fat F.

Jan mumbled something and left me to sulk in peace.

I must've fallen asleep because the next thing I knew Daddy was nudging me. "Mom kept your dinner warm."

They must be worried about me, I thought, sitting up. We had strict rules about eating with the family. Otherwise you didn't eat.

Dad perched on the side of the bed. "So you beat the odds, did you?"

"Huh?"

"You got the word."

"I couldn't believe it! I still don't. I really thought I'd heard wrong. And, of course, I blew it."

He patted my shoulder. "There'll be other spelling bees."

"But, Daddy, I missed it on the first round. It was my very first word! Now Sister Rose thinks I didn't study."

"How do you know that?"

"Oh, I know! I know by the way she glared at me. All that time we spent and she thinks . . ."

"Forget what she thinks."

Now I couldn't believe what I was hearing. Dad telling me to forget what Sister thought?

"Your mother and I know you studied. But more important, you know."

"Could you give me a note tomorrow telling Sister how long I studied?"

Considering a moment, he said, "Spell *restaurant* for me."

"What?"

"*Restaurant*—spell it."

"R-e-s-t-a-u-r-a-n-t."

"Now, will you ever forget how to spell that word?"

"No, never."

"At least you learned one thing from all this. I could write a note telling Sister you studied, but do you really want me to? Your mother and I have never fought our children's battles. Besides, you did misspell the word. You'll just have to work harder to prove to Sister Rose you're a good student."

It wasn't what I wanted to hear. I sat there for a few minutes before asking, "Daddy, do you think people cause the bad things that happen to them?"

"Cause them?"

I fiddled with a loose thread on the bedspread. "We have this new girl in our class, and I haven't been very nice to her, and now bad stuff keeps happening to me."

Dad's eyebrows knitted together. "How haven't you been nice?"

After I explained, he said, "No, I don't think God works that way. But I do think you should try to put yourself in the girl's place. How would you feel if you were new at school and no one talked to you?"

"But, Daddy, she's dirty and—"

He held up a hand. "I didn't say you had to be her friend. Just think about what I said."

I knew he was right—about Eunice, anyway. I knew she was lonely and I'd hate it if nobody talked to me, but Daddy didn't realize what I'd be risking if I became her friend. Everybody would start treating me as if *I* had cooties.

But as I walked into the dining room for my supper, I thought, I don't know why I should feel so guilty about Eunice. After all, she won the spelling bee.

CHAPTER 6

Good Times, Bad Times

I ALWAYS THOUGHT that getting through bad times was easier if you had something fun or interesting to look forward to.

So even though school was horribly boring on Monday, I tried to pay attention, telling myself that choir started in the morning. I almost *had* to pay attention because every time I so much as moved in class, Sister Rose gave me the evil eye. I knew she was remembering the spelling bee.

Somehow, though, I made it through the day without getting into any more trouble and was pleasantly surprised when Sister assigned homework in only two subjects—English and arithmetic. For English, we had to write a 250-word animal story.

"I will be giving other writing assignments

throughout the year," Sister said, "but this one will give me an idea of what you already know about narrative writing."

She turned to the board. "Since this is an animal story, I want you to study your pet, if you have one, then make up a story about it. If you don't have a pet, maybe you could observe a friend's or perhaps you could write about a zoo animal." As she talked, she wrote on the board, WHAT DOES THE ANIMAL LOOK LIKE? HOW DOES IT MOVE? WHAT KINDS OF SOUNDS DOES IT MAKE? PAPERS DUE FRIDAY!

I loved writing stories. We didn't have a pet, but I knew what I'd write about. We had loads of squirrels in our backyard. I watched them from the apple tree.

Anxious to start on my assignment, I raced home after school, changed my clothes, grabbed a paper and pencil, and climbed into the tree. At first I didn't see any squirrels. But after a few minutes I noticed one across the street, playing near the edge of the woods. It picked up an acorn, popped it into its mouth, and scampered over to our yard. I was so busy trying to keep an eye on the squirrel and jot down notes that I lost my balance, bumping and crashing through several branches of the tree. I caught myself on a lower limb with one hand.

I was scraped and bruised, and the squirrel had disappeared.

I didn't have a lot of notes, but because I'd watched the squirrels so often, I decided I was ready to write the story. I hobbled inside.

I titled my composition "Bonny Graysquirrel." I thought the first paragraph was pretty good so I read it to Daddy after supper. *Bonny Graysquirrel perched on the swaying branch of the old oak tree. She wrapped her bushy tail around her, trying to stay warm in the freezing temperatures. She knew she should be looking for food. Oh, how she wished she'd paid more attention when Mama had given the lesson on gathering food for the winter. It was bad enough last winter, hunting for herself, but since her three babies had arrived in June she had them to feed also.*

"Sounds like a good beginning," Daddy said.

Janice, who'd been doing her homework at the table, wailed, "Oh, poor, poor Bonny Graysquirrel! Whatever will poor Bonny do?"

"Daddy, make her stop!"

"Jan, behave yourself."

"But Daddy, I'm *so* worried." She placed the back of her hand up to her forehead and gave an exaggerated sigh. "What'll happen to Bonny's babies if she can't find any acorns? Oh, I know, Arlene can adopt them!" She howled with laughter.

When Daddy started laughing too, I snatched my paper out of his hand and ran into the bedroom.

He came after me. "I'm sorry I laughed. Don't let Janice upset you. You have a fine opening paragraph. Let me read your story when it's done."

I wasn't sure I'd show it to Daddy or anybody. Maybe Sister Rose would think it was silly too. Maybe I wouldn't even finish it. I shoved it into my desk drawer and flopped across the bed.

At least I had choir to look forward to in the morning.

That night as Jan and I were getting ready for bed, she said, "If you want to go with me tomorrow, I leave no later than quarter of eight. Sister Alma doesn't like it when people are late."

"Are you saying I'm allowed to walk with you?" My voice dripped with sarcasm.

"I'm saying you better get up at six-thirty because I'm getting the bathroom at seven."

"I don't have to get up at six-thirty," I told her. "I already took my shower so I'll only need fifteen minutes. You'll be out by seven-thirty. Won't you?"

"How can you get ready in fifteen minutes? I took my bath tonight, too, but I—"

"You're uglier than I am," I said with a dirty laugh, "that's why it takes you longer."

"Ha! Have you looked in a mirror lately?"

I stuck my tongue out at her.

"I don't care what you do," she snorted. "But *if* you intend to go with me, I leave at seven forty-five!" She reached over and flicked off the lamp. In a few minutes I heard her steady, rhythmic breathing.

But, excited about choir, I had trouble falling asleep. I wondered if we'd get to sing songs right away. Would Sister still think I had a very nice voice?

The moonlight shining through the branches of the apple tree created funny patterns on the floor between our beds. They resembled some graphs I'd seen on the board in Jan's classroom. I stared at the swaying designs until I fell asleep.

The next thing I knew, Jan's alarm clock was blaring. It was seven o'clock. She rose immediately. Jan was one of those disgusting people who wake up bright and cheerful, ready to face anything or anybody, even nuns.

Since I knew I wouldn't be able to get into the bathroom until her highness was finished, I turned over, hoping to wake up gradually. I fell asleep again instead.

Suddenly, Jan was yelling, "Arlene, it's seven thirty-five!"

I hopped up, ran in, went to the bathroom, brushed my teeth, and splashed my face with cold water. By the time I threw on my uniform and combed my hair, it was quarter to eight. Jan was gone.

My stomach growled like an angry bear.

As if she'd heard it, Mama said, "You can't go to school without breakfast."

"Well, why didn't you call me?"

"I called you twice and twice you said you were getting up. I didn't have time to come in and yank you out of bed. I was fixing Daddy's breakfast."

Daddy lowered his newspaper and glared at me. "You're big enough to get yourself out of bed, Arlene. Your mother has enough to do around here without giving personal wake-up service."

I grabbed a handful of Wheaties and stormed out, biting my tongue to keep from answering back.

"Took you long enough!"

I jumped. I hadn't seen Jan standing in the shadows of our screened-in front porch.

It surprised me that she'd waited, until I saw what a dreary day it was. The gloomy sky produced a light mist. But over in the woods, patches of fog swirled near the ground, creating a scene from a monster movie.

Jan skirted to my right and said almost in a whisper, "Hurry up."

Apparently she didn't want to be next to the woods. I was going to tease her about being afraid, but I was still too sleepy, even for an argument. Besides, the woods were kind of spooky this morning.

When a squirrel darted out in front of us, we both screamed. Then Jan laughed. "Shame on you, Bonny Graysquirrel, leaving your babies alone on a scary morning like this!"

"Shut up, Jan," I said, "you're just jealous because you can't write."

"Ha, as if I'd want to write squirrelly stories. Oh, come on, Sister hates it when people are late."

We ran the last few yards to the church. The eight o'clock bells rang as we climbed the steps to the loft.

Holding our ears, we sat down. When the bells finished chiming Sister Alma smiled and said, "Good morning, children."

"Good morning, Sister."

"This morning I'd like to tell you what I hope

you, as a choir, will be able to accomplish this year."

I studied her as she spoke. Why did I feel relaxed around Sister Alma? Sister Rose always made me feel the way I did before stepping into the confessional.

"One of the things we need to do today," Sister Alma continued, "is get you seated according to size and the part you're singing."

We jabbered and joked as she moved us around. But she didn't yell. She talked and joked right with us.

When we were finally lined up correctly, Sister said, "Let's be quiet now."

Funny thing was, everyone listened immediately. Then she handed out some sheet music and sat down at the organ. Hands poised over the keys, she was about to play when, from the back of the loft, we heard, "Sister, what about me?"

We all turned around and stared at Annette.

"Yes, uh, what was your name again?"

Sister was usually so good with names. How could she not remember Annette?

"Annette."

"Oh, yes, Annette. What do you mean, what about you?"

Annette's lips formed a pout. "You said I have an in-between voice. What part am I supposed to sing?"

"Oh, I remember you now!" Sister sat there a

moment as if thinking. "Why don't you stand on the end near the door, next to Mary-Kate."

I knew why Sister was placing Annette beside Mary-Kate. Mary-Kate Turner had the strongest voice in the choir. Jan was always talking about how great she was. Mary-Kate would not be thrown off by Annette's *in-between* voice.

"I'm also appointing you our librarian, Annette," Sister said. "When we need a sheet of music, you'll be in charge of getting it for us. I'll show you where the files are later."

Annette's pout immediately changed to the more familiar smug expression.

I snickered. Annette was too stupid to understand why Sister was making her librarian.

We learned a Latin hymn that Sister said we'd probably sing at Mass in a couple of weeks.

When she told us practice was over I was amazed that the hour had passed so quickly. She'd made it fun and interesting. Jan was lucky to have Sister Alma as a teacher.

I bet they laugh all day long, I thought. Then I pictured Sister Rose laughing. Her flawless white skin would probably crack into a million pieces.

Heaving a huge sigh, I trudged over to school to begin another miserable day with china-faced Sister Rose.

But one good thing did happen. Sister Rose gave us a spelling test.

"Even though spelling bees are important," she

said, "I realize that some people become nervous when they have to stand up in front of the class. A written exam may be fairer."

What had gotten into Sister Rose? Trying to be fair? This was certainly something new.

Because I was sure I'd done well on the test, I was in a good mood as Nancy Lee and I walked home at lunchtime.

"Hey, Nance, are you going to write about Rusty for your composition?" I asked.

She stared at me as if I'd asked my question in Swahili.

"You know, the animal story we have to turn in on Friday."

"I don't know," she snapped, "and I don't care!"

"What's wrong with you?"

She didn't answer until we reached my house, then she said, "Let's go into your backyard a minute. I have to talk to you."

Something in her voice worried me.

She sat at the picnic table. I perched on the swing hanging from our oak tree and waited for her to speak. It seemed an eternity before she said, "Last night, I heard my parents talking. I'm sure they didn't want me to know . . ." She started crying.

"Know what?"

"It's Brian. We haven't heard from him in three months."

Nancy's brother was a marine and had been in

Korea about a year. There'd been so much in the newspapers and on the radio about the war in Korea, and, although Sister Rose had explained that it now seemed to be coming to an end, we prayed every morning for the American military over there. Five kids in our class had brothers there.

"But, Nancy, maybe . . ."

"Oh, Arlene, they're afraid he's missing in action or even killed!"

Fun-loving, freckle-faced Brian? He couldn't be dead!

I was afraid. Afraid for Brian, Nancy Lee, and their parents.

Then I got really frightened, thinking about Ed. Could he be sent to Korea after he graduated from high school in June?

"Will you make a novena with me?" Nancy Lee's voice interrupted my thoughts.

"Sure," I answered. Saying a prayer for nine days was easy.

"We'll start tomorrow," she said. "I'll come by about ten of."

"Come by?"

"Don't you want to go together?"

"Go?"

"Daily Mass is at seven."

"Oh," was all I managed to say. She'd been talking about a novena of Masses. Nine days! I'd have to get up nine straight mornings at six-thirty. Even though I hated that thought I couldn't tell my best friend I wouldn't go with her just because I didn't like to get up early. Besides, I knew that if I didn't go and something happened to Brian, I'd feel like it was my fault.

How could life be so good one minute and so bad the next?

CHAPTER 7

Mean Sister Rose

WE BEGAN OUR novena the next day. I felt good afterward because Nancy didn't seem quite as worried. But Nancy never did stay in a bad mood for long.

My good feeling didn't last. In class Sister Rose handed back our spelling tests. I'd only gotten one wrong—*friend*. Though I was mad at myself for missing even one word, I was elated when I saw the big red A at the top until I noticed what Sister had written next to it—"*I* before *E* except after *C*. Shame, Arlene! You should know better."

I saw Eunice's paper then. She'd gotten A+, and beside her mark was written "Excellent work, Eunice!" Apparently Eunice had spelled all the words right.

No praise for me for getting all but one right. Oh, no, Sister Rose had to scold me for the measly one I got wrong.

I was so angry, I tore my paper in half with Sister staring right at me. It made a really loud noise too. But I didn't care.

"What's the matter, Arlene," Annette whispered, "get a bad mark on your test?"

Before I had a chance to answer, Eunice said, "No, she got an A. What did *you* get?"

"None of your business," Annette hissed back, quickly slipping her test paper into a book.

"Quiet, girls," was all Sister said, even though I was certain she knew I'd ripped apart my spelling test.

Having Eunice take up for me made me feel a tiny bit better. But the whole class would have to stick up for me before I'd be able to forget that Sister hated me.

Thursday afternoon, right before the bell, Sister Rose said, "Don't forget, children, your animal stories are due tomorrow."

I told myself I'd forgotten but I hadn't really. The first part of "Bonny Graysquirrel" was still in the desk in my room. I didn't want to finish it, but what else could I write about?

When I got home I pulled out the paper and scribbled down the rest of the story. I'd had it all worked out in my head the other day, so it didn't take long to finish. I wasn't even careful about my handwriting. What difference did it make anyway?

I could write *Moby-Dick* and Sister Rose would find something wrong with it.

I passed it in Friday morning.

Sister didn't give them back for two and a half weeks. During that time I worried. If I got a really bad mark, it would bring my English grade down.

Before she returned them she said, "We'll be having other creative writing assignments during the year. Next month I'll teach the techniques of dialogue. From reading your papers, that's where your greatest weaknesses are."

I held my breath when Sister handed me mine. I'd received a B+. Next to the mark she'd scrawled, "Good story, Arlene, but I had to take off points for sloppiness. Were you daydreaming again when I said neatness counted?"

I felt like screaming. But right then and there I vowed to pay close attention when Sister taught anything about writing. After all, she did say my story was good. If I worked hard, maybe I could win the English award at the end of the year. I usually earned good marks in English, but I'd never won the top honor.

Sister was forever talking about setting goals. The English award would be mine. I'd show that mean old Sister Rose!

Nancy Lee and I were playing jacks on the school steps the next day when a boy from Mikey's class came running over to us. "Your brother fell down and he's bleeding."

Nancy and I raced to a crowd of kids standing in a circle. Mike lay in the center. Sister Rose, kneeling on the ground next to him, held a snow-white handkerchief up to Mike's head. The handkerchief was rapidly turning red.

"Oh, Arlene, help me take your brother inside," she said.

Mike's face was pale and, though his bottom lip quivered, I could tell he was trying hard not to cry.

Sister got to her feet, carefully pulled Mike up, and guided him into the school. I followed.

We rushed down the hall toward the bathroom. When Mike came to an abrupt stop, I bumped into him.

"I'm not going into the girls' room!" he cried.

"Michael," Sister said, "the boys' room is too far away. You have a nasty cut. We've got to stop the bleeding. You would pick a day when the nurse is out sick."

"No, Sister!" he said, and wouldn't budge.

Sister sighed. "Arlene, go into the bathroom, make certain it's empty, then run across the hall for a sheet of paper, write 'out of order' on it, and place it on the door." She lifted Mike's chin. "Will that be okay, Michael?"

He nodded, and after I checked the room he went inside with her.

After doing what Sister had told me I returned to the bathroom. She had Mike sitting on a stool. He was holding one handkerchief on the cut while she washed his face with another. I wondered how many handkerchiefs she carried around with her.

"The bleeding's stopped," Sister said. "Are you feeling better now?"

Mike nodded again, but as he did huge tears began to roll down his cheeks.

I stood there gaping as Sister hugged him. "It's okay to cry, Michael," she said softly. "You've been very brave. As soon as Arlene comes back we'll get you a bandage."

I coughed.

"Oh, Arlene, stay with your brother while I run down to the health room for a bandage. Keep applying pressure to the wound."

I obeyed without a word.

At the door, Sister turned. "I won't be long. And don't worry, it's not as bad as I thought."

My mouth was still hanging open when Mike whispered, "I thought you said Sister Rose was mean, Arlene. I like her."

I didn't know what to say.

CHAPTER 8

Christmas Shopping

"I NEED THREE volunteers to remain this afternoon to decorate the classroom for Christmas," Sister said one Friday morning early in December.

Hands stabbed the air with chants of, "S'ster, S'ster, ooh, S'ster, pick me!"

As Sister surveyed the sea of candidates, I saw that Eunice was one of the few girls who didn't have her hand up. I couldn't imagine *anybody* not wanting to decorate, especially Eunice. I'd noticed her drawing Sister Rose once. The sketch was good but if I'd been doing it, I would've made Sister look like a fire-breathing dragon with blazing blue eyes.

Sister pointed. "Robert Dombrowski and . . ."

"She'll probably choose Annette the pet," I mouthed to Nancy Lee when Sister glanced away.

Sister picked Annette for everything. At least all the good stuff.

Sure enough, she called Annette's name and, to my total surprise, mine!

Had I really been asked? Me—Sister's most *un*favorite person in the classroom, probably the school, maybe even the world?

I bet she feels guilty about choosing her pet, I thought.

But after school she let me decorate the windows, a job we all wanted.

"I'll be working in another room, children," Sister said after she'd gotten us started on our chores. "Please behave yourselves."

Why was she going to another room? Did she think she'd be in our way? I rather doubted that. But I didn't ponder this long. I had a job to do. I gathered my supplies and was about to start when Annette shoved me out of the way. "I'm doing the windows."

"Sister said I could," I retorted.

"So? Do you see Sister anywhere in this room?"

"I'm telling," I said.

Annette laughed. "And I'll tell her that you're making the whole thing up just to get me into trouble. Who do you think she'll believe?"

Before I could come up with an answer Robert said, "She'll believe *me*, Annette. And boy, would I love to snitch on you!"

Annette's face turned as red as Sister's gets sometimes. For a second I thought she might cry, but all she did was stomp her foot and return to the task she'd been assigned.

Robert and I laughed as we began our work. With Glaswax, I made each pane of glass look like it had snow banked along the edge. I printed MERRY CHRISTMAS on the center panes and stenciled snowflakes all around. It took a long time, but as I stepped back to check my creation I felt pleased with the results. Only then did I realize that Sister had come back into the room and I was alone with her, something that made me very nervous. If she was ever going to mention that first day of school when I'd sassed her, now was the perfect time.

"Are you finished?" she asked.

"Yes, Sister."

"You'd better go home then. The others left half an hour ago and it's getting dark."

I grabbed my coat from the cloakroom, collected my books, and headed for the door.

"The windows are pretty, Arlene. Thank you."

Bursting with pride, I smiled at her and had almost reached the hall when she added, "Too bad you don't show as much interest in your schoolwork."

I felt as if I'd been slapped. Did she enjoy being mean to me? Maybe that's why she chose me in the first place—to torment me.

I was so upset, I flew from the classroom.

When I entered the house Janice was wrapping

presents at the dining room table while Mama ironed last year's Christmas paper.

Forgetting the incident with Sister for a moment, I said, "You should see the pretty paper Nancy Lee's mother bought. And they don't save it from year to year either."

"They don't have five kids," Mama pointed out quietly.

She looked tired, and I was sorry I'd made the crack.

"A bike doesn't have to be wrapped," I hinted.

Janice sneered. "What makes you think you're getting a bike?"

"Do you think I will, Mom? It's all I want."

Danny glanced up from his coloring book. "Just ask Santa Claus."

"Santa doesn't always bring what you ask," Mama said. "Sometimes he runs out of items before he gets to certain areas."

"I always get what I want," Mike added, walking into the room.

"All I want is that jewelry box." Janice's voice sounded dreamy. "You know, the wooden one with the red velvet lining. It has two drawers, a place for rings, and—"

Mom unplugged the iron. "I've had enough of 'I wants' for tonight. We have to set the table for dinner. Daddy will be home soon."

After dinner Mom said, "Aunt Gussie's coming tomorrow morning to stay with the boys. Woolworth's is having a big sale. Do you girls want to go? I need at least one of you to help me carry things home on the streetcar."

Before I could open my mouth Janice said, "Margie and I made plans to see that new Humphrey Bogart movie."

"As long as *The Catholic Review* gives it an A rating," Mama replied, "it's all right. I guess Arlene will have to go with me then." She wiped off the oilcloth, then shook a finger at Janice. "But remember, it's your turn to do the bathroom. I better not come home and find out Aunt Gussie did it for you."

I awoke Saturday morning to the smell of cinnamon. Throwing on my robe, I hurried into the kitchen in time to see Aunt Gussie removing a pan of raisin buns from the oven.

She hugged me. "You're up early for a Saturday."

"I smelled the buns. Where's Mama?"

"Hanging up the wash. It's so cold out, I bet it'll freeze before she comes back in."

The house was quiet—something that didn't happen often. Daddy had gone to work hours ago. Jan and the boys were all still sleeping. That meant I had Aunt Gussie to myself, something else that didn't happen often.

She placed a bowl of steaming oatmeal, one of the buns, and a glass of milk in front of me, then sat down with a cup of coffee. "How's Arlene?"

I took a bite of the bun and told her all about yesterday afternoon and Sister Rose. "Do you think when she goes to confession, she tells the priest that she's been nasty to me? Or don't nuns have to go to confession?"

Aunt Gussie chuckled. "Of course they do. But Sister Rose probably thinks she's doing and saying these things for your own good."

"No, she hates me, that's all."

"Maybe she wants you to do better with your lessons."

Adults always stick together, I thought.

Mama came inside then and said she wanted to be at the stores when they opened.

I hated shopping with Mama because she took forever to make up her mind. But I figured I'd better be on my good behavior if I wanted a bike for Christmas, so I didn't balk. I even tried to be cheerful.

Fortunately, the streetcar wasn't crowded on the way over to Hamilton, the local shopping area.

"Who are you buying for today, Mom?" I asked, as she pulled a list from her pocketbook.

"I want slippers for Aunt Agnes, a flannel shirt for Dad, and Woolworth's has Tonka trucks on sale."

After hopping from the streetcar we trekked three long blocks to the stores, going to Woolworth's shoe department first where Mama found the slippers for Aunt Agnes. As if she were trying on a ring, she placed a slipper on her hand and held it away from her. "What do you think?"

"They're pretty. Let's get them."

She checked the price. "Three ninety-nine! I

don't know, that's awfully dear. I think I'll see what Irving's has first."

She bought a shirt for Daddy and a dump truck for Danny—both were on sale.

"What about the jewelry box for Janice?" I asked.

"If I buy one, you have to be quiet about it. Janice has a way of worming things out of people."

"I won't tell."

The gleaming mahogany jewelry box sat high up on a shelf on a pedestal draped with pale blue satin. As it slowly revolved, a pair of rhinestone earrings, resting against the red velvet, sparkled under the lights. I guess if you liked that sort of thing, the jewelry box was pretty.

Mom spotted the price. "Eight ninety-nine— that's ridiculous!" She began examining cheaper boxes on the counter below. The one she selected, pearlized plastic with a pink flower painted on the lid, only cost four ninety-nine. "It serves the same purpose," she said.

Before I could tell her Janice would hate it, Mom was handing money to the clerk.

Poor Janice, I thought, and poor me. If Mama won't spend eight ninety-nine on a jewelry box, I have no chance for a bike.

After comparing prices at the stores across the street, we returned to Woolworth's and Mom bought the slippers. Then we went to the soda fountain for an ice-cream sundae. That was the only good thing about shopping with Mama.

Ice pellets stung our cheeks as we headed back

toward the streetcar stop. After we waited half an hour, the jam-packed streetcar finally came. Mama managed to get a seat but I had to stand. By the time we got home I was tired and grouchy and convinced that Christmas was going to be terrible.

CHAPTER 9

Up in Smoke

THE FOLLOWING WEEK Sister Rose asked for volunteers again. "This job will be a privilege. I need two people to help me clean and polish the brass so the altar will be beautiful on Christmas Day."

This time only a few hands went up. I slid down in my seat. She's not doing it to me again, I thought. But picturing a new bike, I considered what she'd said. Maybe if I did something for the Lord, He'd do something for me. Slowly I inched my hand upward and, like a dog pouncing on a bone, Sister called me. I wondered what terrible things she had planned for me.

She also chose Nancy Lee, so I decided it might not be so bad, after all.

That afternoon we followed Sister over to the

church, and she showed us how to polish the brass. Then we helped her gather all the items to be cleaned. I felt special being in the sanctuary, since girls weren't usually allowed up on the altar.

We returned to the sacristy to work. "I'm going to leave you for a while," Sister said. "I have papers to correct. I'll be back periodically to see how you're progressing."

I was glad she'd left us alone. It was fun since Nancy Lee and I laughed and talked as we polished.

When Sister came back we were each doing our last candlestick.

"Beautiful!" she said. "You girls have done a wonderful job. When you're finished, please go out through the church. I would wait, but I'm already late for dinner and Sister Margaret doesn't like it when any of us is tardy for meals. Thank you, girls."

When the sacristy door closed behind her I heaved a sigh of relief, secretly hoping Sister would be late.

Nancy Lee finished her candlestick before I did and said she'd wait in church. When I joined her she was kneeling by the rack of votive candles in front of Saint Joseph's statue. She dropped a coin in the box marked *offering*, then lit a candle. I figured she was praying for Brian. Her parents had finally heard from him. He was supposed to be home for Christmas. Of course everyone was elated, but Nancy Lee said she wouldn't believe it until he walked through their front door.

In the flickering candlelight Nancy's face resembled one of the saints on the holy cards the nuns were always giving us. They said that when we lit a candle and said a prayer, the smoke somehow carried that prayer to God.

Moving over to the vigil candles in front of the statue of the Blessed Mother, I gazed up. Mary's hands were outstretched. She wants to help, I thought, reaching for the long wick used for lighting the candles.

I lit one, but instead of blowing out the wick I lit another, then another, until every candle burned. In my coat pocket I had the dime for foreign missions that Sister had forgotten to collect. I slid it into the box, then prayed as hard as I could for a bike, thinking, All this smoke is sure to get *somebody's* attention up in heaven. After my prayer, I decided to slip in an extra dime, one I'd brought to buy candy with after school. It was the least I could do, especially if I got the bike.

As I stood up, I wondered if I had looked saintly, the way Nancy Lee had. I wished she were still there to see me, but she'd already gone outside. I did feel kind of peaceful and confident as we headed home.

The next morning when Sister Rose asked Nancy Lee and me to step out into the hallway, that peace and confidence shattered. Sister spoke to Nancy Lee first and, though I couldn't hear what was said, they kept glancing at me.

After Nancy Lee went back into the classroom Sister beckoned to me. Her expression worried me. It worried me a lot.

"What did you and Nancy Lee do yesterday after you left the sacristy?"

I tried to think, but it was hard with those eyes boring into me. "We lit candles," I mumbled.

"How many candles?"

I shrugged.

"How many did Nancy Lee light?"

"One."

"Did she say what she was praying for?"

I didn't think it was any of Sister's business, but I told her that I imagined Nancy Lee was praying for her brother.

"And you!" She made it sound like a dirty word. "How many candles did you light?"

"I don't know. I didn't count them."

"Don't be impertinent, young lady. You lit all of them, didn't you?"

"No, Sister."

"Are you saying you didn't?"

"No, Sister, some of them were already burning."

"And what were you praying for?"

How could I tell her I was praying for a bike? She'd probably tell me it was a sin to pray for *material* things or something awful like that.

"A special intention," I replied softly.

"What special intention?"

Heart hammering in my chest, I stared straight

into those blue eyes and said, "You always told us that special intentions were private."

Cheeks blazing, she clutched the cross around her neck. "Did you put any money in the offering box?"

"Yes, Sister, twenty cents."

"You're supposed to put ten cents in for *each* candle," she cried.

"But, Sister, it says *offering*. Isn't an offering something you do if you want to, not something you have to?"

She turned red all over then, and she couldn't seem to get her breath.

I thought, If she dies, they'll say I killed her!

But finally, she let out a big puff of air and muttered through clenched teeth, "Your parents will be informed of this. You can be certain of that!"

I could see my bike going up in smoke and, somehow, blocking the prayer smoke. I crept back into the classroom.

Mama and Daddy were informed, all right, by way of Janice. "You pea brain, lighting all the vigil candles," Janice said. "How dumb can you get?"

I glared at her, glad now that Mama had bought the ugly jewelry box.

I tried to explain to Mom and Dad that I thought offering meant you could put in whatever amount you wanted—*if* you wanted. I *didn't* tell them I was praying for a bike.

No matter—they still said I was wrong. So the next day I had to take four dollars (my allowance for a month) to Sister Rose for candles. Worst of all, I had to apologize. It just wasn't fair. I'd only lit those candles after slaving all that time on the brass.

Christmas was definitely going to be rotten this year.

CHAPTER 10

Christmas

ABOUT A WEEK before Christmas Sister said, "Some of you have asked about a party." She glanced at Annette. "I always allow my students to pick names for a gift exchange. So it would be nice to have a Christmas party the day we give our gifts."

Everyone started jabbering and Sister had to bang her desk for quiet. She asked for volunteers to bring refreshments.

I knew Aunt Gussie would bake something, but I figured with my luck Sister would break a tooth on whatever I brought. I grabbed on to my desk to make sure my hand didn't accidentally go up.

And, thank goodness, Sister got enough volunteers. Then she turned to the rules for swapping gifts. "You may spend between a dollar and a dollar-fifty. Do not go over that amount. Is that agreeable to everyone?"

Everyone answered, "Yes, Sister." Everyone except Eunice, who didn't say anything.

Sister passed around a box containing all the names. I was hoping to get Nancy Lee's. I sure didn't want Annette or a boy.

When my turn came I closed my hand around one of the slips and pulled it out. My heart sank—Eunice Montgomery.

Lately the Boobsey twins—that's what Nancy Lee and I had nicknamed Annette and Connie—had started calling Eunice *Punice*. They held their noses when they said it. They never said it around her, but a lot of the kids repeated it so I'm sure it got back to her.

Nancy Lee glanced my way now, and when Eunice wasn't looking I showed Nancy the name I'd drawn and she held up hers—Lee Hunt. We both made faces.

"Maybe we can go shopping together," she whispered.

I nodded.

Somehow when I'd shown Nancy Lee my slip of paper Annette had seen, too, because after school she and Connie cornered me.

"You got Punice's name, didn't you?" Annette said, snickering. "Oops—I mean Eunice."

"So? What if I did?"

"So *we're* going to tell you what to buy her," Annette retorted.

"I don't need help from you."

"But it's perfect," exclaimed Connie. "Who knows? Maybe she'll take the hint."

"What are you talking about?"

"Soap—you can get her soap, shampoo, and a washcloth." They screamed with laughter.

"That's mean."

"Why is it mean? Maybe they're just too poor to buy soap. Anyway, you better do it," Annette said, "or you'll be sorry." She whispered something to Connie. They laughed again, then ran off chanting, "Eunice, Punice, never clean, until she gets soap from Arlene."

Why would I be sorry? It would be just like Sister's pet to make up something horrible about me. Of course, as much as Sister hated me, she'd believe Annette and add it to the long list of bad things she already had against me.

"Do you think her family *is* too poor to buy soap?" Nancy asked after I told her.

"But a bar of soap doesn't cost much," I said.

"Oh, those two. As if they're perfect! I sure wouldn't listen to them. What can they do anyway?"

I shrugged. Did I dare take a chance on finding out? It was one thing to ignore Eunice, but what the Boobsey twins were suggesting was downright nasty. I couldn't—no, I wouldn't do that to Eunice. But what was I going to do?

Since Nancy hadn't really been any help, I thought about asking Mama or Aunt Gussie what I should do but I knew what they'd tell me. I could almost hear Aunt Gussie saying, "Never do anything that will hurt you or someone else."

I even considered seeking Sister Alma's advice, but the only time I saw her was at choir practice. And with Christmas quickly approaching, our rehearsals were so busy that she didn't have time for anything but music.

I worried for a few days and put Nancy off about shopping. Now, with only two days left, I told her we'd go tomorrow. I was so desperate, I even sat in my thinking place, hoping the tree would inspire me. It didn't.

That night as Janice and I were getting ready for bed I guess I must've acted worried because she said, "What's wrong with you?"

Could Janice help? Would she? Janice washed her face and hair more than anyone I knew. She'd probably tell me to go ahead and buy the soap.

Before I knew it I was explaining everything. And for once Jan didn't make fun of me or call me stupid.

"Her brother's in my class," she said. "His name's Charles. He's kind of square, but he's really smart—quiet too. Some of the kids made fun of him in the beginning."

"Why?"

"His shirt's always wrinkled like he's worn it all week, and his pants have patches on the knees. I think he only has that one pair. One day we both stayed after for make-up tests. Remember when I had the grippe? Anyway, when we were leaving, I asked him if he'd had the grippe too."

"What did he say?"

"He said no, that his baby brother was sick. He'd had to stay home with him." Jan stopped brushing her hair for a moment and looked at me. "Stupid me—I asked him where his mom was and he said she'd died in June."

I gasped. "But Eunice never said anything. What did she die of?"

"I don't know. All Charles said was she'd been sick for a long time, and they moved here so she could go to a doctor at Johns Hopkins. He also said there were six kids in the family."

I sat there stunned. Eunice had lost her mother in June, had come to a new school in September, and nobody talked to her. I was such a horrible person for treating Eunice the way I had. Jan hadn't ignored Charles just because *he* wasn't dressed immaculately.

Tears dribbled my cheeks. "Jan, I should've been nicer to Eunice. I do like her even though I didn't want to in the beginning. What am I going to do about a present? I can't make things worse for her."

"Oh, punch that snooty Annette in the face. Her sister's in my class and she acts just like her."

"Then she'll run to Sister Rose."

"When are you going shopping?"

"Tomorrow afternoon."

"Maybe I'll come up with something before then."

We got into our beds and Janice turned out the light. My head had scarcely hit the pillow when she asked, "Arlene, did Mom buy me a jewelry box?"

"You know I can't tell you that."

"I've got to know! Margie and I are giving each other earrings, I think Aunt Agnes might've gotten me a bracelet, and I hope you're going to get me one of those new pop-apart necklaces. Remember, I want blue." She sighed. "It's so humiliating, keeping my jewelry in a cigar box. Besides, it gets all tangled. If I get a jewelry case, I'm going to put it under the lamp on my dresser so light will shine on it the way it does in the store." She sighed again, more dramatically. "Tell me if I'm getting a jewelry box, and I'll tell you a secret."

"What secret?"

"Tell me first."

"Jan, I promised Mama I wouldn't say."

She switched on the light again. She was smiling like a Cheshire cat. "This secret is about Lee Hunt."

Mama would kill me if she found out I told. Of course, Jan wasn't receiving the jewelry box she wanted, but her question was, Was she getting *a* jewelry box?

It was sort of a dirty trick, but I whispered, "Yes, Mama bought you one. Now tell! What about Lee?"

She let out a little squeal then confided, "He smokes."

"Cigarettes?"

"No, cucumbers. Of course cigarettes."

"How do you know?"

"I saw him. He was with a couple of high school boys. They were *all* smoking. And they were doing it right behind school. If Lee ever got caught, he'd be kicked out of St. Anthony's." She laughed. "Of course, that might be the only way he gets out."

I laughed, too, and turned out the lights.

When I woke the next morning, Janice had already left for school. I vaguely remembered her mentioning that she was going early to help Sister Alma redo the bulletin boards.

But I saw a big note propped up on the bureau. All it said was BUBBLE BATH! Suddenly I felt light as air. What a great idea!

Nancy Lee bought a Duncan yo-yo for her gift and I found a jar of bubble bath on a half-price table in Read's drugstore. It cost $1.19. I wrapped it in some cute paper with snowmen on it and Janice made a pretty red bow for it.

When we exchanged gifts in school the next day Eunice didn't open hers right away. She just sat staring at it. For a moment I didn't think she was going to open it at all. But then she cautiously removed the paper, being extra careful not to crush the bow. Her face lit up when she saw the bubble bath.

Annette was watching too. I glared at her, daring her to say something. She just stuck her nose in the air, shrugged, and turned away.

I tore into my gift then—a pretty charm bracelet

from Maria Lusco. Jan would probably try to con me out of it.

Some kids always gave gifts to the teachers. I never did. And I certainly wouldn't have given one to Sister Rose! I saw brownnoser Annette hand her a big box. What in the world did you buy a nun? I wouldn't find out because the nuns never unwrapped their gifts in front of us.

At dismissal time Sister distributed boxes shaped like little suitcases, filled with hard candy.

Even though we'd just had cupcakes, cookies, and punch, most of us, me included, started devouring the candy immediately. Eunice held hers tightly as if she was afraid someone would snatch it from her.

"Boys and girls," Sister said, "I want to thank you for all your cards and gifts. I hope you have a happy, blessed Christmas, and while you're away, please stay safe in the bosom of the Christ Child."

Apparently Sister didn't hear Lee snicker at the word *bosom* because she added with a smile, "See you next year!"

We were noisy as we filed out of the classroom, something Sister wouldn't have permitted ordinarily.

Outside, Eunice caught up with me. "I love the bubble bath, Arlene, thanks. The jar is so pretty, I wish Mama . . ." She stared at the ground.

I didn't know what to do. Should I say I was sorry about her mother? "Maybe you could come over and play sometime during the holidays," I said finally.

She smiled, her eyes shiny. "Oh, I'd love that but I don't know. I'll probably have to watch my little brothers a lot."

I scribbled my phone number on a piece of paper. "If you want to, just call." I paused. "And have a merry Christmas." Then I thought, How can she have a merry Christmas with no mother? And here I am worried about a bike.

My unselfish thought didn't last long because the closer Christmas got, the more I wondered just what I was getting. I knew the bike was out, but I hadn't mentioned wanting anything else.

It was a madhouse at 5404 Greenhill Avenue on Christmas Eve. My screaming little brothers chased each other around the dining room while Janice and I wrapped last-minute gifts on one end of the table and Mama rolled cookie dough on the other. She'd already burned one pan, and the smoke hung in the air the way it does in church after Father incenses the altar.

"Santa Claus isn't even going to *come* to this house," Mama shouted.

Danny stopped a minute as if thinking about that, but Mikey smacked him and they were off and running again.

Mama sighed. "Why do children automatically act like little devils right before Christmas?"

Somehow the slow day ended, and it was time

to hang up our stockings. Mike had gone through
Dad's sock drawer twice trying to find the biggest,
settling for a stretchy black one. Mine was gray,
Danny's brown, and Janice's and Ed's were argyle.

After we finished and Mom shut the double
doors between the living room and dining room, the
stockings hanging on the fireplace were the only hint
in the room that tomorrow was Christmas.

When we went to bed Mom also closed the doors
separating the bedrooms and bathroom from the rest
of the house, something she didn't usually do.

I read "The Night Before Christmas" and the
story of the first Christmas to Danny and Mike until
I knew each by heart. Mike fell asleep first, but at
ten o'clock Danny was still wide-awake.

He squirmed in his bed. "Leeny, I don't think
Santa's going to bring me anything."

"Why?"

" 'Cause I've been naughty."

I laughed at his use of the word *naughty*. "Oh?
What did you do?"

" 'Member when Mama said I had to eat my
brussels sprouts?"

"You ate them, didn't you?"

"No, I dropped them behind the radiator. Now
Santa's not going to bring me anything."

I tried not to laugh. "Oh, I think he will. What
he'll probably do is cut out one of the little toys he
was going to leave."

"But, Leeny . . ."

I sighed. "What?"

"I bopped Mikey with my beanbag."

"Danny, don't worry. Just go to sleep. I promise, Santa will bring you stuff." I tucked the covers around him for about the tenth time. "But he definitely won't come if you're still awake."

He squeezed his eyes shut, and though I knew he wasn't asleep I went downstairs.

Janice was already sleeping. She'd polished her bureau until it shone, leaving a big space under the lamp for the jewelry box.

I crawled into bed, wide-awake. Moonlight splashing through the branches of the apple tree created milky puddles on the floor. "The moon on the breast of the new-fallen snow . . ." played over and over in my head with snatches of, How will Janice act when she sees that ugly jewelry box? until I fell asleep.

The next thing I knew, Danny was shaking me and Mikey was shaking Janice. "Come on, get up," they said, "it's Christmas." I glanced at the clock—six A.M.

Janice and I grabbed our robes and jumped up. The house was freezing. We hurried into our parents' room, where they both snored loudly.

Mikey nudged Mama, who woke instantly. When she informed Daddy that it was morning already, he groaned. "You kids crawl into our bed while Daddy goes down and throws some coal in the furnace," Mom said, shrugging into her bathrobe.

I could feel Janice trembling next to me. "Are you getting sick? You're shivering."

"No, I'm just excited. What's taking them so long?"

I tried to get up enough nerve to warn her that she wasn't getting the jewelry box she wanted. I couldn't.

After what seemed like hours Mom and Dad said we could come in.

The living room had been transformed into a Christmas wonderland. The tree in the corner, strung with large colored lights, glass balls, and tinsel, was the most beautiful I'd ever seen. A Christmas garden occupied the space under the tree. A five-car train chugged through a snow-covered miniature village containing tiny houses, stores, street signs, animals, and people.

By this time Ed had joined us, and the five of us stood in the doorway taking it all in until Danny spotted his dump truck and Mikey saw his baseball glove.

"Hey, Arlene," Mike said after a few moments, "here's your bike."

I thought he was kidding, but sure enough, in the corner, partially hidden by the tree, stood a bike. I ran to it. It wasn't new but it had been painted a shiny blue. It had new handle grips with strips of plastic flowing from them, a new seat and mirror, and a gleaming chrome bell.

I was so surprised, all I could do was gape. Then I noticed Jan rummaging through the presents. She picked up a package big enough to be the jewelry box.

I felt guilty and wished I'd told her she wasn't getting the nicer one.

I couldn't watch. Straddling my bike, I gazed into the fireplace, heard the hiss of the gas logs, Danny making truck noises, and Mike thumping the baseball glove with his fist. Then I heard the *r-rip* of paper and Janice saying, "Oh."

I held my breath.

"Oh, thank you," she said, "it's even more beautiful than I remembered."

I spun around. Janice cradled the wooden jewelry box in her lap. I didn't understand. I glanced at Mama, who gave Daddy a knowing smile. She must've taken the plastic one back. Then I did something really strange. With tears rivering my cheeks, I rushed over to Janice and threw my arms around her. "Oh, Jan, I'm so glad you got the one you wanted."

Then an even stranger thing happened. Jan didn't push me away or call me dumb; she hugged me back. "And I'm glad you got your bike!" We both laughed.

Boy, did I love Christmas!

CHAPTER 11

Best Friend

EUNICE PHONED FRIDAY morning of our week-long Christmas holiday. "Daddy's home with a bad cold today," she explained, "and the babies are sleeping. He said I could go out for a while." She paused. "Is it all right if I come over?"

"Sure," I answered, trying to sound pleased. I liked Eunice, but what would we do? I didn't really know her.

I called Nancy Lee, hoping she could play too. Then I remembered that she'd gone to her grandmother's. Her family was upset because Brian hadn't made it home for Christmas. "And after Dad spent the whole day putting up the welcome sign," she'd said.

When Eunice got to my house I saw that she'd ridden a bicycle. It was pretty beat-up.

"Want to go riding?" I asked. "I got a bike for Christmas."

"Sure," she said, "but I have to go home when I hear the noon Angelus bells."

We headed over to LaSalle Avenue, a really hilly street in the neighborhood.

"Let's pretend we're detectives chasing criminals," Eunice shouted as we sped down a steep incline.

"Yeah, and one of the bad people is a . . ." I almost said *nun*, but stopped myself. I wasn't sure Eunice would think that was funny.

The cold wind stung our faces as we flew over the hills, but I hardly noticed, I was having so much fun!

We rode till our legs burned. Then we heard the bells.

"I have to go," Eunice said.

"Not already."

"We've been playing for more than two hours, and I promised Daddy I'd be back around noon so I could give the boys lunch."

It sure hadn't seemed like two hours. "I hope you'll be able to come again," I told her, and this time I meant it.

"It's a good bit warmer since the sun came out," Eunice said. "Maybe Daddy'll let me take the boys for a walk after lunch. Would you like to go with me if he says it's okay?"

"I'd love to," I said, thrilled. I still liked baby dolls. I'd never admit it, though, because I was too old. But playing with real babies was different. It didn't matter how old you were!

I went home, ate lunch, and waited. Eunice phoned just as I finished eating. We made arrangements to meet halfway between her house and mine.

Boy, were her little brothers cute! Eunice had them so bundled up, you could barely see their faces. The youngest ones were twins. They sat in a big double stroller. Another little boy walked next to her, holding on to the stroller.

"You can help push if you want," Eunice said. "The twins are Spencer"—she pointed—"and that's Steven. And this big guy is Billy."

The big guy beamed at me.

"How old are they?"

"The babies'll be two on January twenty-ninth. Billy's three and a half."

As we ambled through the neighborhood, I made believe *I* was the mother. Eunice was just a friend visiting me. But when Spencer got fussy and Steven cried for Mr. Bear, Eunice said she'd better take them home.

Eunice was lucky to have babies around all the time.

It had been a great day. I'd almost reached my house before remembering there was more fun in store. Jan was sleeping over at Margie's tonight, and Mama had agreed to let Nancy spend the night with me. We were going to have one last blast before school started again.

When I entered the bedroom Jan said, "Nancy Lee wants you to call." She paused. "She sounded strange."

"What do you mean?"

"I don't know. Nancy's always so cheerful. She seemed kind of upset."

"Oh, God, I hope nothing's happened to Brian," I said, rushing into the living room. As I dialed I whispered a quick prayer. "Hi, Nance, what's up?"

"I'm surprised you found time to call me," she snapped.

"Why wouldn't I? Aren't you sleeping over tonight?"

"You mean you still want me?"

"Of course! What's wrong with you, Nance?"

"Me? There's nothing wrong with me. I just thought maybe you'd rather have your new best friend instead."

"I don't have a new best friend."

"You don't?" Nancy's voice rose. "Well, it wasn't *me* you spent the day with. *I* don't have any baby brothers for you to play with."

What's with her, I thought but said, "I phoned you this morning to see if you wanted to play with us. You weren't home. Didn't you go to your grandmother's?"

"Yeah, but Grandma wasn't feeling well. We only stayed about an hour. I saw you from the car.

You two were having so much fun on your bikes. Then later . . ." She paused. "You did call me?"

"Yes, I didn't want to play with Eunice by myself. We had fun, though. I like Eunice. But, Nance, *you'll* always be my best friend."

Nancy was quiet for such a long time, I thought maybe she'd hung up. When she finally spoke I could tell she was crying. "First Brian didn't come home, then I thought you didn't like me anymore."

"Oh, Nance, I'm sorry. I don't have to play with Eunice if you don't want me to."

Nancy was silent again before she said, "Do you think your mom would let Eunice spend the night too?"

I wasn't sure about that, but I *was* sure Nancy was the best friend anybody could ever have!

CHAPTER 12

✤ —————————————————————— ✤

Ladies in Waiting

WHEN WE ENTERED the classroom that first school day in 1952, I saw that my artwork had been erased from the windows as if Christmas itself had been scrubbed from the calendar. On the bulletin board, instead of the manger scene and "For Unto Us A Child Is Born," we now had snowflakes surrounding HAPPY NEW YEAR with "Sing Unto Him A New Song" written underneath.

There were lots of announcements. One that I didn't want to hear was that there would be no choir practice this week. Maybe Sister Alma thought we'd appreciate an extra week off from singing. Our Christmas Mass had been beautiful. She'd been very pleased.

Sister Rose was explaining some complicated

long division problem on the board when someone knocked on the door. This didn't happen often because everybody knew Sister Rose hated interruptions.

When the door opened I saw Mrs. Monahan, the housekeeper for the rectory, standing there. Every time I saw her I thought of how Daddy had said she looked like a sack tied in the middle.

Sister stepped out into the hallway to talk to her. Whatever it was about, she didn't seem pleased. Finally I heard her say, "Very well, but please be expeditious.

"Children, I believe you all know Mrs. Monahan," Sister said when she came back into the classroom. "She has a proposal for you."

"St. Anthony's Parish has a turkey-ham supper every year," Mrs. Monahan began. "The ladies of the Sodality do the cooking, and usually the seventh- and eighth-grade girls act as waitresses. Unfortunately, this year the dinner was scheduled without first checking with Sister Alma. It seems the eighth grade is going on its school trip that day and won't be home in time to help with the dinner.

"Because of this I am relying on our sixth- and seventh-grade girls. I'll also need two or three big, strong boys. I'll pass around a sheet of paper. Any of you who would like to work, please sign your name. We'll have a meeting the Friday before the supper to instruct you in your duties."

Before she could pass the paper Sister stopped

her. "Mrs. Monahan, I'd prefer that they check with their parents first."

"But I wanted to get this taken care of today," Mrs. Monahan snapped.

"We still have a few weeks until the supper. They can talk to their parents tonight. Now please excuse us. We were in the middle of our arithmetic lesson." Sister picked up the chalk and began writing on the board.

Mrs. Monahan stood there a few seconds with a shocked expression on her face before storming out.

Wow, I said to myself, I thought *I* was the only one Sister Rose got mad at!

I loved the idea of helping at the dinner. Janice had made fifteen dollars in tips last year. She'd have a fit when she found out she wouldn't be able to do it this time and I would. I knew exactly what I'd buy with the money too. My roller skates were hand-me-downs and a wheel had fallen off in August. Daddy had said he'd try to fix them, but he hadn't.

"Waiting tables isn't easy," Janice said that night at dinner. "Some of the people treat you like their slave. My legs hurt for days afterward."

"Can I, Mom?" I asked, ignoring Janice. "Sister said we have to have our parents' permission. I can do it. I know I can."

"I suppose it'll be okay, but you'd think someone could've checked before scheduling the dinner, so the older girls would've been available."

"Yeah, it makes me mad!" Janice griped. "But I

know what happened. Margie's mother was at the Sodality meeting when the women were planning the dinner. She said Mrs. Monahan just marched in and announced that the dinner had been set for January nineteenth. She'd already had the fliers printed. Some of the ladies got real upset. They'd just voted to change the date to February ninth to give them more time to sell tickets and so they could decorate the hall in a Valentine's Day theme."

Mom shook her head. "That Mrs. Monahan— just because she's Father Fitzsimmons's cousin she acts like she runs the parish."

Janice laughed. "Margie's mother said they should list *her* as pastor instead of Father."

Mama chuckled. "Oh, I suppose she means well."

Most of the girls did get permission to serve at the dinner. I couldn't wait, especially since Woolworth's was having an after-Christmas sale and all roller skates were half price until the end of January.

Time dragged before the dinner.

Nancy Lee, Eunice, and I had become good friends since that night we had the sleep-over at my house. We made plans to wear navy blue skirts and pink blouses for waitressing. We all had the skirts, and Nancy was going to lend a blouse to Eunice. We were also going to fold a fancy handkerchief and pin it to our blouses the way the waitresses did at Read's.

The day before the supper we met with Mrs. Monahan in the hall. Some seventh- and eighth-grade boys were setting up tables. Mrs. Monahan had to shout over the noise. Finally she said, "Come into the corridor."

Thirty girls crowded around.

"First of all, girls, I expect you all to be here promptly at two-thirty tomorrow. The doors open at three P.M. I think it would look nice and be less confusing if you wear your school uniforms. You'll be given aprons."

Most of us groaned, but I heard Eunice say, "Darn." Mrs. Monahan ignored us.

Nancy Lee inched her way beside me and poked me in the side. "Ask about the tips."

Taking a deep breath I raised my hand. Mrs. Monahan nodded at me.

"My sister worked last year," I muttered. "Quite a few people left tips. Do you think—"

"Shame on you! You should be grateful just for the opportunity of helping your church." She paused, heaving a sigh. Her huge bosom seemed to rise up at least a foot and, for one crazy moment, I pictured the forklift at Daddy's store. "We will handle tips differently this year," she said in a nasty tone. "They'll be put into a box I'll provide. Then the money will be divided."

"But that's not fair!" I blurted.

Mrs. Monahan scowled at me. "And why isn't it fair?"

I gulped. "Well, if one person works real hard and somebody else just goofs off, why should they get the same amount of money?"

"Yeah," Annette and three seventh-graders chimed in.

"There will be no goofing off. I will see to that." She smoothed back her sparse gray hair, told us a little about how to serve, then said, "All right, see you tomorrow at two-thirty. Don't be late."

Nancy Lee, Eunice, and I had almost made it to the door when Mrs. Monahan said softly but quite distinctly, "And I'll be keeping a close eye on *you*, Miss Warren."

I cringed. Why was it that everybody seemed to know my name? Here I was, getting away from Sister Rose, and now I had Mrs. Monahan to worry about. Why did things like this always happen to me?

The next day when I walked into the hall, things got worse. In the kitchen, helping with the cooking, stood Sister Rose!

For the first hour and a half, everything went fine. I'd even put five dollars into the tip box. Nancy Lee, Eunice, and I had gotten tables in a row. Nancy had contributed three dollars to the box and Eunice had added four.

Serving wasn't too hard either. We gave plates of ham, turkey, and stuffing to people when they sat down, then carried bowls of mashed potatoes, sweet potatoes, string beans, and gravy to the tables. We had to keep the roll basket filled. If anyone wanted coffee or hot tea, they could help themselves, but we served the cold drinks.

Mrs. Monahan had said one of the bigger boys would be working the cold drink counter.

"I didn't know you'd be here," I said to Lee when I saw him behind the counter.

"I didn't know I'd be here either," he snickered, "but you know how persuasive *she* can be."

At first I didn't know he was talking about Sister Rose.

I laughed and gave him my order of two Cokes, two iced teas, and a milk.

Lee scooped ice into four paper cups, filled two with Coke, poured tea into the others, and hung lemon slices on the rims of the cups. Grabbing a pint bottle of milk, he plunked everything down on my tray.

I carefully lifted the tray, turned, and bumped smack into Father Fitzsimmons.

Ice, Coke, milk, and tea flew everywhere. When the metal tray clattered to the floor, it sounded like an atomic bomb exploding. I swear, at that moment everything in the hall came to an abrupt standstill.

Forks paused halfway to people's mouths. Conversations stopped mid-sentence. The girls carrying food halted in their tracks. Even the screaming baby shut up. And they were all staring at me!

I could feel the blood rushing from my toes all the way up until my face burned with embarrassment. "I'm s-sorry, F-Father," I stammered, chasing ice cubes and trying to keep the puddle from spreading. Horrified, I noticed a chunk of ice in the cuff of Father's pants leg with a lemon slice perched next to it, standing as crisp and straight as it had on the cup of iced tea seconds before.

Just as I reached for it, Father stepped away. Then I saw another pair of legs approaching—fat ones! Still on my hands and knees, I spun around and tried to make a getaway but plowed headfirst into the folds of a long black skirt.

Trembling, I got to my feet. Sister Rose was standing next to Mrs. Monahan, whose eyes blazed. "Look what you did to Father's suit," Mrs. Monahan snarled.

"Now, don't blame her, Estelle," Father said. "I wasn't watching where I was going."

I glanced at Sister Rose.

"Maybe you'd better get a mop, Arlene," she said calmly.

I ran as fast as I could, biting my lip to keep from crying.

When I'd returned, Sister and Lee had picked up all the ice. Mrs. Monahan was busy dabbing milk spots from Father's suit.

Lee winked at me as he took the mop. "It *was* the old coot's fault," he whispered.

Even though I was shocked at Lee's name for Father, I couldn't help giggling. All of a sudden Lee didn't seem quite so bad.

Sister handed me the tray. "Get some more drinks. You don't want to keep your customers waiting."

That was all she said. No *How could you do such a thing?* or *Be more careful in the future.* She didn't even frown. This was certainly a day full of surprises.

I didn't drop or spill anything else for the rest of the evening.

Our next-door neighbors came to the supper and chose my table. After they'd eaten, Mr. Ryan slipped me a five-dollar bill. "You were a good waitress, Arlene. Here's something for your trouble."

I glanced around. Neither Mrs. Monahan nor Sister Rose was anywhere in sight, and none of my classmates seemed to be paying attention.

Mr. Ryan had said it was for *my* trouble. No one would know if I put the money in my pocket. Then I saw Nancy Lee lugging bowls of steaming vegetables to her table. Little beads of sweat had popped out on her upper lip and across her nose. Her curly hair clung to her forehead. It looked like someone had taken a crayon and framed her face with red circles. She caught me staring at her and smiled.

Reluctantly, I trudged up to the tip box and dropped in the five bucks.

Then I realized something. I hadn't seen Annette for quite some time. She was supposed to be serving the table next to Eunice's. But now Eunice was working hers and Annette's. Where had Annette gotten to?

I served my last dinner around eight-thirty. Janice had said her legs had hurt for days. I couldn't even feel mine. My back ached and my feet were swollen. At least it was over!

I wondered how much we'd made in tips. I'd contributed at least twenty dollars to the pot.

The ladies were cleaning the kitchen, and some men had started to fold up the tables.

Sister Margaret saw us milling around. "You can go on home now, girls. You did a marvelous job. Thank you."

We all just looked at each other. Then I noticed the tip box—*didn't notice* is more like it. It was gone and so was Mrs. Monahan.

"Was there something you needed?" Sister Margaret asked.

"We were wondering about our tips," I told her.

"Oh, yes, I'm sorry. Mrs. Monahan said she was taking the box over to the rectory. She'll divide the money and get back to you in a day or so."

All that hard work and now we had to wait for our money. It's nothing but highway robbery, I thought, and pictured Mrs. Monahan skulking over to the rectory with the loot under her arm, cackling like a witch.

CHAPTER 13

And Waiting
and Waiting...

ALL DAY MONDAY I kept expecting a knock on the classroom door. Where were our tips? I couldn't seem to think about anything else.

Once, Sister asked me where my mind was. If we didn't get the money soon, the sale at Woolworth's would be over, and if I didn't pay attention, I'd be in even deeper trouble with Sister Rose.

On the school ground Thursday morning, a seventh-grade girl asked if I'd heard anything. Before I knew it, most of us who'd worked the supper were standing in a circle.

"I think we should *do* something," someone said.

"But what?" said Nancy Lee.

"Maybe we could ask Sister Rose or Sister Alma to help us," Eunice offered.

We quickly voted that idea down.

"Maybe she absconded with it," I said. "We should just go over there and ask for our money. After all, we earned it!"

"Let's go," they all shouted.

"Wait a minute," Eunice said calmly. "She might think we're ganging up on her if we all go."

"Yeah, you're right," Nancy said, and suggested three from each class.

"Any volunteers?" I asked.

Silence.

"Since it was your idea, Arlene," one of the older girls said, "I think you should go."

"All right. Nance, will you come too?"

She nodded.

I glanced at Eunice.

Before I could ask if she wanted to go, Annette spoke up. "I'll go. That Mrs. Monahan really has a nerve keeping our money!"

I suddenly remembered Annette's disappearance at the dinner. "How long did you work at the supper?"

"I worked plenty!" she fired back.

"Well, you're not going over to the rectory with us. Eunice will."

"I bet you all get into big trouble for bugging Mrs. Monahan," Annette whined, before stomping off.

The older girls selected their three people, but because it was almost time for the bell, we planned to meet again after lunch.

All during the history lesson I rehearsed in my

head what we should say. "Mrs. Monahan, we were wondering if you've had time to count the money." Maybe she can't count, I thought, smiling to myself. "Mrs. Monahan, remember the tip money from the supper *almost a week* ago?" "Okay, Mrs. Monahan, fork over the dough right now!"

The lunch bell rang.

I ran home, practically inhaled my food, then rushed back. At school, we chose Carolyn Koerber from seventh grade to do the talking. Then our little group tramped over to the rectory.

As we climbed the steps my heart pounded. But on the porch we were all afraid to ring the bell. Finally Eunice knocked.

Nothing happened. Maybe Mrs. Monahan *had* absconded with the loot. Suddenly the door flew open. Mrs. Monahan squinted at us through the storm door. She looked like she'd been sleeping.

"What do you want?"

We stood like statues.

"I don't have time for jokes, girls. What is it?"

Carolyn slipped behind the group and nudged *me* forward. Now Mrs. Monahan took notice. She even opened the storm door. "Oh, yes, Miss Warren!"

I cleared my throat. "Um, Mrs. Monahan, we were wondering if you've had time to count the tip money." I fixed my eyes on a mustard stain on the collar of her ugly, flowered dress. "I mean it's been almost a week. Of course, um, we know you're busy and everything, but . . ." I was rambling.

"Yes, I have been busy," she snarled, "and no, I haven't had a chance. When I do, I'll bring the money over!" She slammed the door in our faces.

"She really steams me!" Carolyn said as we trooped from the rectory.

"I bet she spent it!" Nancy Lee cried.

"She'll probably make us wait another week just for spite," I grumbled. "And I won't be able to get my roller skates at half price."

Friday afternoon, shortly before dismissal, someone rapped on the classroom door. Sister asked me to get it. I was shocked to see Mrs. Monahan because I figured we wouldn't be hearing from her for at least another week.

"I want to speak to Sister Rose," she hissed.

I'm dead meat, I thought.

When I told Sister that Mrs. Monahan wanted to see her, Sister sighed, finished what she was writing, put down her red pencil, then slowly strolled toward the door, which she left ajar about six inches.

Every girl in the room watched that door.

I could make out snatches of Mrs. Monahan's side of the conversation—"audacity, impugning my character." And as plain as day, I heard her say, "that Warren girl."

Sister's voice was just a murmur, but when she returned, carrying a stack of envelopes, her face was flushed—the way it gets when she's angry.

The bell rang. Sister said, "I'd like the girls who served the church supper to please stay."

For a few minutes there was confusion—announcements from the P.A. system, the rest of the class shuffling out, people going back and forth in the hallway, and outside, someone clapping erasers. Then stillness. It seemed like an hour of stillness before Sister said, "I want to say something about your performance at the supper."

Here it comes, I thought, not daring to look at anyone.

Sister got up, came around in front of her desk, and hoisted herself up. She actually sat *on* the desk with her feet dangling!

"When Mrs. Monahan said she wanted you girls to work, I had my doubts because waitressing is hard work. I know because I waited tables in high school." She crossed her ankles and began swinging her legs slightly.

Amazed, I sneaked a peek at Nancy Lee, who was gawking at Sister with her mouth wide open.

Sister went on, "But you girls were friendly, courteous, and efficient. I don't think the eighth-grade girls could've done any better."

She smiled, jumped down from the desk, and started handing out the envelopes, calling names as she did, "Jane, Eunice, Arlene, Maria, Nancy Lee, Annette—ah yes, Annette, as I recall, you developed a terrible headache about a half hour after the dinner started. You said it was a *migrant* headache, I believe?"

"Yes, Sister," Annette replied, putting on a pitiful face.

Sister opened Annette's envelope, pulled out a

dollar, and gave it to her. "I think that's a fair share for the time you spent. The remainder of this will be divided among the girls who worked all day. I'll check to see how many seventh-graders there were, then I'll give the rest of you your share on Monday."

I was astonished! Could I have been wrong about Annette being Sister's pet?

"Well, thank you, ladies, you can go now."

I didn't move, figuring Sister would probably want to yell at me about the spilled drinks or asking Mrs. Monahan for the money.

"Did you need something, Arlene?" Sister asked after everyone else had gone.

"No, I just thought you'd . . . No, Sister!" I rose and made a beeline for the door.

"Arlene."

Ah-ha, I knew it! "Yes, Sister?"

"Now that you've finally gotten your money"— she emphasized *finally*— "do you have plans for it?"

Was this a trick question? Maybe I should say I was going to put it in the poor box—nah, she'd never believe that. "Roller skates!" I said almost defiantly.

"Good choice. It's been a long time since I skated, but there's nothing like it, is there—speeding down a steep hill with the wind in your face. . . ." She paused to gaze out the window, and I pictured Sister roller skating down Greenhill Avenue, her veil flying in the breeze. She continued, "And after you take off the skates your feet feel all tingly and funny. Good exercise too." She smiled at me. "Well, you enjoy."

"Yes, Sister." I turned to leave.

"But, Arlene—"

"Yes?"

"Be careful."

I nodded, too shocked to speak. What was happening? This wasn't the Sister Rose *I* knew.

In the dim, quiet corridor, I thought about the last half hour. I glanced back into the classroom. Sister was still at her desk, staring out the window. She looked kind of sad. Janice said she figured Sister Rose was only in her twenties. Maybe she's wishing she could go skating again, I thought.

Remembering the envelope, I tore it open and started counting. Twenty-two dollars! Enough for the skates with plenty left over for a couple of double-dip hot-fudge sundaes topped with whipped cream, nuts, and a cherry.

CHAPTER 14

The Holy Terror

ONE DAY EARLY in February Nancy Lee's mom called in the morning to tell me not to wait for Nancy. She wouldn't be going to school. I assumed she was sick, so after supper that night I phoned to see how she was.

In the background I heard music and people talking. "You don't sound sick," I said.

"I'm not. Mom just let me stay home." Her words rushed with excitement. "Brian's home! He got here around two."

I felt hurt that she hadn't told me, and I let her know.

"We've had so many false alarms. Mom didn't want to jinx it by telling anyone until Brian walked through the door. He was so glad to be home, he lay down on the living room floor, spread his arms and legs like someone making snow angels, and kept saying, 'I can't believe I'm actually home.' Mom was bawling, of course. We would've all started crying except Rusty came charging in, jumped on top of Brian, and licked him."

I laughed. "I'm really glad he's home, Nance. Tell him I said hi."

"I will. Oh! Guess what else he said?—and these are his words: 'The Holy Terror wrote to me at least once a month the whole time I was over there.' "

"Holy Terror?"

"Don't you remember? That's what Brian used to call Sister Rose when he had her in eighth grade. He said Sister's letters got him through some tough times. She never once mentioned she was writing to him. It sure was nice of her—wasn't it?"

"Yes, it was," I mumbled. Brian had *hated* Sister Rose when she was his teacher. She must've known that, yet she wrote all those letters to him. Sister could be a holy terror, but she *did* do nice things. The longer I tried to figure her out, the more confused I became.

"What are you going to give up for Lent, Eunice?" Nancy Lee asked as we all headed to St. Anthony's on Ash Wednesday.

Eunice had started walking with us occasionally. Her brother would wait with her till either Nancy or I showed up.

Nancy thought it was sweet the way Charles looked out for Eunice. But I had a sneaking suspicion that he was interested in Jan, and this gave him an excuse to walk to school with her.

"I'm giving up drying dishes," I said, laughing.

"I think I'll give up brussels sprouts," Nancy exclaimed.

"But you hate brussels sprouts," I shouted. We shrieked with laughter.

"I'll give up baby-sitting, cooking, and . . ." Eunice's words dissolved into a fit of giggles, "and changing poopy diapers!"

"Pee-Uuu," we cried.

By the time we got there I'd narrowed down my *serious* list to candy and movies. Nancy and I figured that if one of us gave up movies, both of us had better do it.

But during the Ash Wednesday Mass, Father Fitzsimmons changed my mind. He said that although it was beneficial to our souls to *do without* something for Lent, often it was more beneficial to *do* something we didn't like. "Why not pick the most difficult?" he'd asked.

I didn't have to think long about my hardest thing. So that morning, ashes still on my forehead, as I marched from church to school, I promised to pay closer attention to Sister Rose during *all* subjects.

Surprisingly, as the weeks of Lent passed I found geography and history kind of interesting. In history we were studying the American Revolution. At one point, while talking about Thomas Jefferson, Sister looked up from the textbook, chuckled, and said, "This is something you might find amusing, class. I read a book of letters once, written by a woman who lived in colonial times. She kept referring to Thomas Jefferson as Tommy Jeff."

If Sister would tell us more stuff like that, I thought, instead of just facts and dates, history wouldn't be so bad. I wanted to hear more about that book. Maybe I'd ask her the name—if I had enough nerve.

I also paid strict attention when Sister taught arithmetic. But it didn't help. I still hated it!

A couple weeks before Easter, at the end of choir rehearsal, Sister Alma said, "Time is running out, children. We need to concentrate harder on our Easter music. There was much too much chitchat today."

Sister had changed that day's rehearsal from morning to after school, but she never told us why.

Even though Sister Alma hardly ever scolded anybody, she'd stopped practice several times to do just that. And she seemed grouchy, which wasn't like her at all.

"Since Annette is absent," she said, "I'll need help putting away the music. Do I have any volunteers?"

I didn't really feel like hanging around, but Sister

looked kind of tired so I raised my hand. Two other girls raised theirs too.

"Collect all the music," she told us, "and bring it downstairs."

When we entered the music room there were several folders on a table.

"Put each piece in numerical order before you file it away."

Each person in the choir was assigned their own number. That way, Sister had explained, if a piece of music was lost, she'd know who was responsible.

When everything was put away we started to leave. I'd just made it to the door when I heard Sister say, "Oh, no."

I turned. "Is something wrong, Sister?"

She smiled but somehow it wasn't her usual smile. I almost asked if she was all right.

"I just left my wrap up in the loft," she said, sighing.

"Would you like me to get it?"

"That would be lovely," she said. "Sometimes those steps . . ."

I didn't wait for her to finish the sentence. I ran up the winding staircase, grabbed the shawl from the organ bench, and barreled down.

"Thank you, Arlene." She threw the shawl around her shoulders. "You'd better go now. I worry about you children walking home in the dark. That's why I prefer morning practice."

She walked with me toward the rear of the church. I held the door for her but she shook her head. "You go on, dear. I think I'll slip inside and make a little visit before I head over to the convent."

I watched her disappear into church. Instead of leaving, though, I quietly followed as far as the doors and peered inside. Sister was sitting in a pew near the middle of the church. I don't know why or how long I stood there staring at her before I went home. It was really strange, but I was almost afraid to leave her alone.

I nearly forgot about the incident until the following week when Jan and I arrived for practice and Sister Rose was at the organ instead of Sister Alma.

"Children, I'll be taking over for Sister Alma until after Easter, possibly longer. With all her many duties, Sister Alma just doesn't have time right now."

I groaned. I thought I'd done it inwardly but apparently I hadn't. Sister glowered at me.

"Sister Rose is just as much a holy terror at choir practice as she is in our class," I griped to Jan as we hurried over to school, "all work and no play."

I overslept the following Tuesday morning.

"You're going to be late for practice if you don't get up," Jan said.

I sat up on the side of the bed but made no attempt to get dressed.

"I'm not waiting for you," she called after a while. Then I heard the door slam.

I didn't go to practice. I know I should've gone and counted it for Lent as one of the things I didn't want to do, but when I joined the choir it was because Sister Alma was the director. If she couldn't keep up her end of the bargain, then neither could I.

As I was leaving for school, Mama asked me to take out the trash.

In class, Sister Rose questioned me about why I hadn't been to rehearsal. Without batting an eye, I said, "I had to help my mother."

She studied me a moment, murmured "Hmm," then turned her attention to arithmetic.

That night Jan asked, "How come you told Sister Rose you had to help Mama and that's why you weren't at practice? You know that's a fib."

"I did so help Mama!"

"What did you do?"

"If you must know, I took out the garbage."

"Oh, Arlene, grow up. That wasn't why you didn't go to choir."

"How do you know what I told Sister Rose, anyway?"

"She came to my classroom this afternoon and asked if you had to stay home to help Mama. This morning she wondered why you weren't there. I told her I didn't know."

"What did you say when she asked if I had to help Mama?"

Jan paused. "I said not as far as I knew."

"Thanks a lot. I'll come to your rescue someday too."

"You wanted me to lie to a nun?"

"I wouldn't have ratted on you!" I shouted and knew I wouldn't have, even if I had to lie to the Pope! Besides, I thought, I bet even the Pope would've had a hard time *always* telling the truth to the Holy Terror.

CHAPTER 15

Secrets

I DECIDED NOT to talk to Jan for at least a week. After all, I might say something she could use against me. It was obvious she couldn't be trusted.

Most of the time Jan wouldn't care beans that I wasn't speaking to her. She probably preferred it that way, but—and this was a big but—Jan hated it when *she* felt like talking and I ignored her.

That's exactly what happened on the third day of my silent treatment. We were in our bedroom getting ready for bed. She'd asked me something, and I acted as if she wasn't even in the room.

"I don't know why you're being such a drag," she snapped, sticking cotton balls between her toes. We weren't allowed to wear fingernail polish to school but, as Jan said, the nuns weren't about to check toes.

I answered with a shrug.

"Do you really think I should've lied to Sister Rose?" she asked, trying to get a rise out of me.

I shrugged again.

"Oh, you're impossible! Okay, maybe I should have told Sister I didn't know why you weren't at practice. I guess that would've been the truth. Sort of."

I wondered what Jan would've done if Sister had been asking about Jan's best friend, Margie.

Jan hobbled over to her dresser for nail polish remover. Halfway back to the bed, she stopped. "Since you're not talking to me, maybe I won't talk to you."

I shrugged a third time.

"Wel-ll . . ." she drew out the word, "if I'm not speaking to you, I can't tell you a secret."

Turning my palms upward, I raised my eyebrows as if to say, So what?

"That's up to you, but this secret is about Sister Alma."

She had me! Thinking about that day in church with Sister forced me to break my silence. "What about her?"

"Ha! Thought you weren't speaking to me."

"So? I changed my mind. What about Sister Alma?"

Wearing a mysterious smile, Jan sat back on the

bed, slowly removed the top to the polish remover, dabbed some on a cotton ball, and bent over her toes.

Even though she was dying to tell me, she was going to make me wait. That was okay. I had plenty of time.

Finally she said softly, "Nobody's supposed to know this, but Sister Alma had a slight heart attack."

"What?"

"She's okay. But that's why we've had a substitute in class and why she hasn't been directing choir. I overheard Sister Celeste when I had to go to the office. She was on the phone. When she realized I'd heard, she asked me not to say anything because Sister Alma doesn't want everybody worrying about her. Sister Celeste said the best way for Sister Alma to recover quickly would be for her to know school and choir were running smoothly."

At that moment I promised myself that I wouldn't miss any more choir practices.

I kept my promise, but it wasn't easy. I *hated* practice with Sister Rose. We had to keep absolutely quiet except when we were singing, and when we *were* singing she never seemed satisfied. Even Jan said she didn't like Sister Rose as director.

But Holy Week finally arrived. Jan and I were hurrying to church for our last rehearsal before Easter. There was no need. We were early. We'd been leaving at least ten minutes ahead of time for choir because we didn't want to get yelled at for being late.

After a grueling rehearsal Sister said, "I'll see you all at seven o'clock Friday evening. Please be on time. Since we're not allowed to have organ music on Good Friday, we'll need to go over things a cappella before the service."

We stood up.

"Just a minute," she said. "Sunday, when everyone went down for communion, it sounded like a herd of elephants. Please be quiet on Friday. Good Friday is a time for reverence and silence." She emphasized *silence*, and as she said it she turned and stared straight at me.

I shivered. Recalling last Good Friday made my arm hurt where Sister Rose had gripped it that day. More than that, I had an awful feeling in the pit of my stomach that this Good Friday was going to be just as bad!

After a Good Friday dinner of potato pancakes and cinnamon-sugar rice, Jan and I headed up to church.

I told myself not to think about last Good Friday. I was afraid if I did, I'd laugh and Sister Rose would have my head. She'd probably be watching me like a hawk tonight. I'd have to be very careful.

We tiptoed up to the loft and took our seats. Once everyone arrived we went over the music for the evening. Then Sister Rose held her finger to her lips as we waited for Father Fitzsimmons to enter the sanctuary.

I tried to pray but kept remembering last year. Glancing down into the church, I noticed Eunice and Charles up toward the front and—oh, no, I couldn't believe my eyes! Even though she was with Brian and her parents, Nancy Lee was sitting in almost the exact same spot as last year, and two pews ahead sat an old lady. I didn't know if it was the same old lady, but . . .

I will not think about it, I repeated silently.

Mass began. As long as we were singing, I was okay. But when Mass was almost over, I panicked. We'd be going downstairs in a few minutes for the veneration of the cross. That was when the priest held a large crucifix and everyone knelt to kiss it.

Suppose someone in the choir has crackly knees? I thought. My heart bounced around like crickets had taken up residence there. Oh, please, please, let everyone have quiet knees.

The choir began to file down. As I reached the spot where the steps narrowed, my heel caught in the hem of my robe. I tripped. With arms waving, I tumbled, bouncing off choir members, whacking the sides of the staircase, and thudding with bone-jarring force along the steps. I was so scared—not of being hurt, but of all the noise I was making.

Halfway down, someone grabbed me, stopping my fall. "Sister's coming." It was Jan. She quickly brushed me off, straightened my robe, then gave me a nudge. "Hurry! Get back up in line!"

Now aware of the pain in my head, shoulder, and hip, I limped back up and got into place just before Sister Rose appeared.

"What was that noise?" Sister hissed.

Silence.

"What was it?"

No one said a word. I was amazed. The whole choir was keeping my secret—even Annette!

Sister stood there, fixed a suspicious gaze on me, then turned and disappeared downstairs.

Trembling like a wet puppy, I forgot about cracking knees *and* Sister Rose as the rest of the service passed in a haze.

"Are you all right?" Jan asked once we were outside and well away from church.

I drew in a shaky breath, hobbled to the curb, and sat down. "I think so." I put my face in my hands and let the tears flow.

Jan took off her jacket, threw it around my shoulders, and sat next to me. We stayed that way for a good while.

Finally I stopped crying and looked up. In the glow from the street lamp I saw Jan's concerned face. "Thanks," I mumbled, smiling.

"What for?"

"For helping me and not telling Sister."

"Well, you didn't fall on purpose. Besides, Sister Rose is a holy terror sometimes."

My smile broadened. Jan and I would still hate each other lots of times, but I was pretty sure we'd never stop loving each other. In spite of everything, it had turned out to be a *good* Friday after all.

CHAPTER 16

How Could You, Sister Rose?

"I SURE AM GLAD we didn't have choir practice this morning," I said to Nancy Lee as we walked back to school the Tuesday after Easter. "Even though we were off I didn't have much of a vacation from Sister Rose."

Nancy laughed. "Why do you dislike her so much?"

I shrugged. If it wasn't obvious to Nancy just how much Sister Rose hated me and was always picking on me, then my explaining wouldn't do any good.

I was tired after the days off and couldn't seem to pay attention to anything Sister taught that morning. But when she said, "We are going to talk, once again, about creative writing," I snapped out of my trance.

At least half the class moaned, but I sat up straighter.

"If you remember," Sister continued, "before Christmas we discussed how to write dialogue and in February we handled plot. Some of you did very well with those assignments."

I smiled. I'd gotten an A on each one.

"Today we're going to discuss writing description. You handled some description when you did your animal stories. But today I'd like to concentrate on describing people.

"When describing a character, either real or fictitious, you must first picture that person in your mind. You should show how the person talks and walks, the kind of gestures he uses." Sister wrote some examples on the board. "For instance, when mentioning someone's eyes, you tell color, but shape or size might also be important. That's what helps to differentiate characters."

She faced the class again. "Right now, as an exercise—this won't count as a grade—as a matter of fact, you don't even have to put your name on your paper—in one hundred words or less, I want you to describe *me*."

Now I groaned along with everyone else!

But I figured as long as she couldn't tell who wrote the piece, I could put down anything.

I began with, *Sister Rose has pretty blue eyes that*

---

seem to change color according to her mood. They bore into you when she's angry. Sometimes she's really mean. Then I pictured her helping Mikey the day he fell, and I remembered that she'd been pretty nice at the supper when I spilled the drinks. And she'd written all those letters to Brian. So I added, *But she can be nice when she wants. She has favorites in the class, though, and I don't think that's right, especially for a nun.*

I knew this wasn't what Sister wanted, but since it wouldn't be graded, who cared? I continued with, *Sister fiddles with her rosary beads when she's nervous and when she's mad her face gets red as a—*I started to say *beet* but that was one of those cliché things Sister had warned us about. I changed it to, *when she's angry she looks as if she has a sunburn.*

I needed a closing sentence but couldn't think of anything. When the recess bell rang I scribbled, *Maybe someday Sister will like all her pupils the same.*

At recess Nancy Lee asked, "Wasn't it hard writing about Sister? She told us we didn't have to put our names on the paper, but I bet she knows everybody's handwriting."

I felt as if I'd swallowed a brick—sideways! How stupid could I be? Of course Sister would know our handwriting!

I trembled as we filed back into the classroom. Sneaking a peek at Sister, I tried to assess her mood. Her face wasn't red so that was a good sign. But her lips were kind of pinched, as if she'd just sucked on a lemon.

132

The papers were stacked in front of her on the desk.

"Your descriptions of me were"—she paused—"enlightening."

Since I wasn't sure if that was good or bad, I gazed at my hands opening and closing in my lap.

"I've chosen a few to read out loud. Then we'll analyze them." She selected one from the top of the pile. " 'Sister Mary Rose has eyes as blue as a summer sky and a voice as clear as St. Anthony's church bell on a cold night.' "

"Though I wouldn't necessarily agree with the writer, the piece is well written." She grabbed another sheet from the stack.

My heart raced.

"I'm only going to read part of this," she said. " 'Sister fiddles with her rosary beads when she's nervous and when she's angry she looks as if she has a sunburn.' "

I held my breath.

"Now whoever wrote this could've just said—when she's angry her face gets red. Similes and metaphors *always* improve writing. Try to remember that."

I couldn't believe it! Sister didn't seem upset by my paper at all. In a roundabout way she'd even complimented it. Today was turning out okay.

Then Sister got up from the desk, turned toward the board, and printed ASSIGNMENT. "For your assignment you will write a description of a person and a place."

Annette put up her hand.

"Yes, Annette?"

"I'm going to write about my father. He's the president of Carrolton Savings and Loan, you know." Her curls bounced as she talked. "Then I'll describe his beautiful office in the bank. It has a big expensive desk and . . ."

Oh, shut up, you pill, I thought. I would have loved to put bubble gum or tar or something even worse in those perfect curls.

I was still inventing awful things for Annette when Sister said, "No, you will not write about your father. You'll be writing about a fellow student. I'm going to appoint each pupil a partner. The partners will write about each other, and they'll describe a room in that person's house."

Annette's hand went up again, but Sister ignored it.

"Since it will be necessary to spend some time with your partner, I'm going to give you three weeks to complete the assignment. The manuscript must be at least five hundred words, but no longer than one thousand." She looked around. "If there aren't any questions, I'll pass out sheets of paper with the names of your partners."

If I get Annette, I thought, I'll slit my throat.

Sister handed me a folded-up slip of paper. I glanced at it and screamed in my mind, Oh, no, how could you, Sister Rose? I stared at the name again just to be sure. I was going to have to describe Eunice—poor, grubby, disheveled Eunice.

There wasn't any way I could write a paper that was honest enough to earn a decent grade and still keep Eunice as my friend.

Every time I started to think Sister Rose wasn't so bad, she'd do something like this. I knew I'd have to tell this in confession, but right now, I hated her more than I'd ever hated anyone.

CHAPTER 17

Eunice

I AVOIDED EUNICE for the next few days. I knew it was stupid because eventually we'd have to get together, but I just didn't know how I was going to write about her.

When I'd finally made up my mind to talk to her, she never seemed to be around. Suddenly it hit me—she was avoiding me! Maybe she didn't know how to write about me either. Or maybe she was afraid of what I'd write.

The next morning Eunice and I made eye contact on the school ground then slowly drifted toward each other.

"Could I come over to your place this afternoon?" she asked. "We need to talk about our creative writing homework."

I agreed, and when we entered the house later the smell of baking bread welcomed us. I remembered that Mama had said Aunt Gussie would be there when I got home. Since Mama didn't drive, she and Daddy were taking Danny to the doctor for a checkup. He was just getting over whooping cough.

"Hello, girls," Aunt Gussie said.

I introduced Eunice and told Aunt Gussie we'd be in my room.

"I want some notes on you," Eunice said as we plopped onto the beds.

We gazed at each other and then wrote things down—things like color of eyes and hair, shape of mouth, and so on. Every once in a while we'd burst out laughing. It was hard to keep a straight face staring at each other that way.

Eunice had pretty eyes. Her hair wouldn't have been bad either if it hadn't been so greasy. But Eunice's teeth really turned my stomach. They weren't decayed or anything, but they had a film on them as if they hadn't been brushed in a long time.

Once, Nancy Lee and I had talked about Eunice's appearance. We thought we should say something to her about it, but we just didn't know how to do it without hurting her feelings.

After a few minutes, Aunt Gussie brought in a snack. "Would you like to stay for supper, Eunice?"

"Oh, no, ma'am, I have to be home by four so my sister can go to work."

We glanced at the little alarm clock on the bureau. It was already twenty after three.

As we munched on homemade chocolate-coconut cookies, Eunice kept taking notes about me and the room.

I was dying to see what she'd written. I only had three things about her—eyes, hair, and shape of face. I guess I could've said her teeth were nice and straight, but with all that gunk on them . . .

Suddenly Eunice took out a clean sheet of paper and I could tell she wasn't writing anymore.

I giggled nervously. "Are you drawing me?"

She nodded. "If I have a sketch, it'll be easier for me to write about you."

I loved Eunice's voice. If I closed my eyes, I could almost see her dressed in a hoopskirt, sitting on the porch of a southern plantation.

At quarter of four Eunice rose to leave. I waited for her to say something about my coming to her house, but she didn't. Never once in the time since Eunice, Nancy Lee, and I had become friends had Eunice invited us over.

As Eunice shrugged into her coat, which had a big tear under one arm, Aunt Gussie came out of the kitchen carrying a bag. "Since you can't stay for supper, I packed you a loaf of the raisin bread I just baked and some more of the cookies."

"B-but don't you need the bread?"

Aunt Gussie laughed. "Oh, no, I always make at least six loaves."

"Thank you," Eunice said softly, then added, "Thanks for having me, Arlene." Clutching the bag of goodies close to her, she left.

I don't know why, but Aunt Gussie and I stood there a long time watching her walk away.

"That's a lonely little girl," Aunt Gussie commented as we closed the door.

"Did Mama tell you that her mother died?"

"No, but I had a feeling it was something like that."

"Aunt Gus, what should I do?"

"About what?"

I explained about the composition. "I don't want to embarrass her," I said. "I'm so mad at Sister Rose for doing this to me."

"Oh, I'm sure she has her reasons."

I should've known Aunt Gussie wouldn't be any help. She'd *never* say anything bad about a nun. Come to think of it, Aunt Gussie never said anything bad about anybody.

For the next couple days every time I got anywhere close to Eunice, she disappeared.

Guess she doesn't want me to come to her house, I thought. But it made me angry. How did she expect me to write *my* paper? Well, maybe I'd just go ahead and put in the stuff about her crummy teeth and *make up* a description of her house.

The Friday before our paper was due, Eunice caught me on the school ground before the bell rang. "Would you like to come over today?"

I almost said, "It's about time!" But instead I told her okay.

She really didn't live that far from me, but it was way past a wooded area that didn't have many houses. We went by some places I'd have called shacks. When I saw the first one I got a sick feeling, thinking maybe it was Eunice's.

"My house isn't so great," she said. "It was okay when we first moved here and Mama wasn't feeling too bad, but now . . ." She paused, then said in an angry voice, "I don't know why Sister had to give us such a dumb assignment."

"I know what you mean," I answered, understanding exactly why Eunice didn't like the assignment. It only made me worry more.

Her home looked like a row house that had been yanked out of the middle and plunked down by itself. The sound of wailing babies greeted us when we walked through the front door.

Eunice threw her sweater over a banister already piled high with clothes, dumped her book bag on the floor, and hurried toward the source of the screams.

I followed her to the back of the house, into a big, bright kitchen. Pretty yellow curtains hung at the windows but the shades underneath were torn. One had come loose from its roller and dangled to one side. A mountain of dirty dishes lay in the sink.

Spencer and Steven sat in high chairs. Their red faces were streaked with tears and their noses dripped. When I got closer I could tell at least one of them needed changing.

"Hey, guys, you remember Arlene, don't you?"

Billy, playing on the floor with blocks, looked up and smiled, but the twins howled even louder.

"Where's Amy?" Eunice asked.

"Upstairs, getting dressed for work," Billy answered, getting up. With finger outstretched, he stuck out his bottom lip and came over to Eunice. "Eunice, my finger has a boo-boo. Give it magic."

She pulled him onto her lap, hugged him, kissed the finger, then wrapped her hand around it. "Uh-oh," she said, laughing, "I feel it. The magic's working. Yep, the boo-boo's all better."

He smiled, jumped down, and went back to his blocks.

"Now which one of you guys needs changing?" she said to the babies. "Spencer, I think you need it worse." She lifted him out of the high chair. "Be right back, Arlene," she called over her shoulder.

From the other room I heard her talking softly to the baby. When she returned, she put Spencer on the floor then took care of his twin. Soon they were jabbering and playing contentedly with each other.

"It's about time you got home." A girl about seventeen or eighteen burst into the kitchen wearing a waitress's uniform. "I thought I'd have to go in late. I—" She noticed me. "Oh, I didn't know you had company."

"Amy, this is Arlene," Eunice said. "We're working on a school project together."

"Hi, Arlene. Listen, Eunice, the twins just got up from their naps. They might want some juice or something. Spencer felt a little warm so I gave him some baby aspirin. I think he might be teething." She pointed to a pot on the stove. "That's beef cooking for stew. It already has the onions and celery with it but you need to add carrots and potatoes and make sure you add plenty of them." She slipped into a jacket. "Oh, yeah, Dad's staying late at the mill again. He said we could use the money. Charles should be home in time to help you give the kids supper and put them to bed. I've got to go." Waving a hand, she rushed out.

Probably glad to escape, I thought. No wonder Eunice looks the way she does. She doesn't have a minute for herself.

Eunice sighed and glanced around as if thinking, What'll I do first? "I'll have to take care of things while you write your notes."

"Can't I help?"

"You better just get your notes."

I took out my pad and jotted down a few things, but mostly I just watched Eunice. It was like watching Mama or Aunt Gussie. She peeled the carrots as fast as Aunt Gussie would've.

She really didn't have time for me and I felt in the way, so I didn't stay long. And once out of there, I couldn't wait to get home to Mama.

Even though I understood why Eunice was the way she was, I still had no idea what to write.

By the time I reached my house I'd decided the only thing to do was tell Sister I couldn't write the piece. Maybe if she knew the reason, she'd let me describe someone else.

But over the weekend, I chickened out. Knowing

Sister Rose, she'd probably give me a failing grade if I told her I couldn't do the assignment as given. And I was *not* going to do anything that would hurt my A in English or ruin my chance at the English award.

I thought about almost nothing else for the next couple of days. On Thursday Sister said, "Don't forget, class, your creative writing assignments are due tomorrow." And as if she knew I hadn't done mine yet, she gazed right at me.

After dinner that night I finally sat down and wrote about Eunice. I asked Mama if I could use her dressing table instead of working in the dining room with everybody else.

I had no idea what I was going to write, but once I started, I wrote the paper straight through, read it, corrected spelling and grammar, then copied it over in ink.

I usually asked Daddy to check my assignments. But this time I knew if it was terrible, there was no way I could redo it.

I passed in the composition next morning then tried to forget about it. I couldn't.

A week later Sister said, "Your descriptive works were, on the whole, pretty good. Some were amusing, some showed potential, but some were disappointing."

I couldn't look up, afraid she might be staring at me.

"I'm not going to hand them back until next week

because I haven't finished grading all of them," Sister said, "but I'd like to read a few aloud. I chose these three because they're so different."

As soon as Sister started reading the first one, we all knew it was about Lee. It was funny, but it didn't make fun of him and the description of his house was really good.

"Nice work, Jane," Sister said. "The only criticism I have is that you don't have a title. But since I didn't specifically say you had to have one, I won't take off points."

I heard sighs of relief.

"The second composition is by Robert Dombrowski," Sister continued, and I immediately recognized Nancy Lee's living room.

I sneaked a peek at her. She blushed, and as if on cue Sister read, " 'And when she blushes, her freckles get bigger and brighter, but nothing could be brighter than this girl's smile.' "

Nancy's probably dying inside, I thought. I'd always suspected that Robert had a crush on her. I guess this clinched it.

"The third paper, called 'The Magician,' was done by Arlene Warren."

My paper! Sister was going to read my paper. Suddenly I couldn't recall one word of what I'd written.

Oh, please don't let it be horrible, I thought, and please don't let Eunice be embarrassed.

"This is a good title," Sister remarked. "Titles

are important, children, because sometimes we select what we're going to read by a title. For instance, given a choice between something called 'Joe Blow' or 'The Magician,' I think most of us would choose 'The Magician' to read. Don't you agree?"

I heard Lee mumble, "Nah, I'd like to find out about 'Joe Blow.' "

Even though I shot him a dirty look, I felt good inside. Sister had complimented my title.

When she began to read my work I remembered that in the beginning all I did was tell about Eunice's kitchen with the sunny yellow curtains hanging at the window. Of course, I didn't mention the dangling blinds or dirty dishes in the sink or anything like that. Actually, I hadn't been too pleased with that part of the composition, but Sister's crystal-clear voice made the room sound like something out of a magazine.

I looked at Annette. She had a surprised expression on her face. Did she really expect me to say Eunice's house was roach heaven? Chuckling, I gave her a triumphant smile.

Then I glanced at Eunice. She seemed nervous, probably afraid of what was coming next.

I held my breath because the second part of the paper contained the description of Eunice. The one sentence I really liked was, *Her eyes are the color of the pale violets that grow wild in the yard.*

When Sister read that, Annette snickered. I could've strangled her. Suddenly I wished that I'd had to describe Annette. I would've said *her* eyes were the color of stinkweed with a personality to match!

In my closing paragraphs I portrayed Eunice as a magician because that's what she'd seemed to me that day at her house. I related the incident with Billy's boo-boo and mentioned how everything seemed to change magically when Eunice entered that kitchen.

When Sister finished reading, Eunice turned and gave me a big smile. Then, unbelievably, so did Sister Rose! "Very fine job, Arlene," she said.

Oh, boy, if hearts could sing, mine would've made the top ten on the radio at that moment.

CHAPTER 18

No More Sister's Dirty Looks

"NO MORE PENCILS, no more books, no more Sister's dirty looks!" Mikey chanted at the breakfast table.

I couldn't believe the last day of school was finally here and, more unbelievably, I'd survived! "No more Sister Rose's dirty looks," I said, laughing.

Jan stared at me with a devilish grin on her face. "For *this* year, maybe. What about next year?"

"What about next year?"

"You could get Sister Rose for seventh grade too. She taught Eddie and me in seventh grade, don't forget. And once she even taught eighth." She snickered. "You'll probably have her for both seventh *and* eighth."

"God wouldn't *do* that to me," I cried.

Jan giggled. "Wanna bet?"

"I hate you, Jan!"

"Me?" She laughed harder. "What have *I* got to do with it?"

"You've ruined my whole summer before it's even started, and you did it on purpose. Now I know I'll get Sister Rose for seventh and eighth!"

"Oh, for heaven's sakes, Arlene," Mama said, "you make Sister Rose sound like a monster. She's always seemed very sweet to me. I don't think you dislike her as much as you pretend."

"I guess I don't dislike her as much as I used to. But I don't think I can take another year of her picking on me." I finished my breakfast in silence. I would *not* spoil my last half day of school by worrying about what might happen. The last day was always fun. We didn't have to wear our uniforms and usually got to play games and goof off. Of course, I didn't know what we'd do in Sister Rose's class.

It seemed funny to see everyone in street clothes as we filed into a naked classroom. That seemed funny too. Empty bulletin boards, no papers being displayed, and blackboards cleaner and blacker than they'd been all year.

One thing did strike me as odd, though. The geography map was pulled down. Wouldn't it just be like Sister Rose to teach something new on the last day of school? But how could she when we'd already turned in our books?

Sister smiled. "Boys and girls, this has been a fruitful, rewarding school year. You've worked quite diligently." She paused. "Well, most of you have."

I sighed. Why was it, after all this time, one glance from Sister Rose still made me feel as if she'd caught me committing a mortal sin?

"I am glad to announce," Sister stated, "that *everyone* has passed to the seventh grade." She stared at Lee and her smile broadened.

We all cheered.

So Lee had finally made it out of sixth grade. Oh, no, that meant he'd be in my class next year too!

"Before I hand out the report cards," Sister said, "I have several achievement awards to distribute." She picked up papers from her desk. "These awards are for the highest grade in a subject."

Maria Lusco received the award for religion. She did almost every year. Maria wanted to be a nun and was the holiest kid in our class.

"The geography *and* history honors go to Nancy Lee O'Reilly," Sister said. "Good job, Nancy."

Everybody congratulated Nancy as she went up to collect her certificates. She looked really cute in her poodle skirt and the green cardigan buttoned down the back.

"Outstanding in art is Eunice Montgomery."

I cheered and was surprised that almost everyone else did too. Eunice had spruced herself up. Her hair was clean. She'd even curled it. Her clothes, though not exactly in style, were wrinkle-free. But what impressed me most were Eunice's teeth. It was obvious she'd been brushing them. I had noticed that she'd been looking neater lately. It made me really happy, but I did wonder whether someone had said something to her about her appearance.

"The next honor goes to our top student in English," Sister went on.

Boy, did I want that award! My heart pounded so hard, I was certain everyone could hear it. The only person who could possibly beat me out was Eunice. I wasn't sure what she'd gotten on the paper she'd written about me. I did know that, like me, most of her English grades were A's.

Oh, please, please, I thought.

"Our top student in English this year is—Arlene Warren."

Surely I'd daydreamed my name, but no, Sister was looking right at me and she was smiling! I was too dumbfounded to move.

"Arlene, don't you want your certificate?" Sister asked.

"Oh, yes, Sister."

Everyone laughed, then they applauded.

I was glad I'd swiped Jan's pearl collar to wear over my blue sweater. This is probably what it feels like to be Miss America, I thought, walking up to the front. I had to restrain myself from bowing.

When I sat down Sister said, "For arithmetic we have—Annette Carlson."

As Annette moved forward a few people clapped politely. She tried to smile but there was such a difference in the praise everyone else had received and Annette's. I mean, it was *so* obvious that I sort of felt sorry for her. I guess because I was still elated about my award I was in a generous mood, so I clapped, too, but not very loud.

Sister smiled.

She sure was doing a lot of smiling today. Maybe she was just as glad as we were that it was the last day.

"Now, children, just for fun, I'm passing out a crossword puzzle. The answers are all spelling words from this year. I'll give a prize to everyone who completes it correctly." She distributed the puzzle, glanced at her watch, and told us to begin.

I might have known Sister Rose would give us something like that to do and call it fun. The explanation to *1 down* was *an eating establishment*. I shuddered, remembering that disastrous spelling bee.

I finished the puzzle in twenty minutes. The prize was a holy card with a picture of Saint Anthony on the front and a prayer to him on the back. Big deal!

With only a few moments left before the bell, Sister told everyone to put away the puzzles. "Before I let you go I have something to tell you." She stood next to her desk, one hand fiddling with a pencil.

What was it? Sister Alma had come back and told everyone she was fine. She was thinner, but she looked great. I didn't think it could be about her.

"As you know," Sister began quietly, "when a woman becomes a nun, she takes a vow of obedience. Which means she does as she's told and goes where she's sent." Sister moved over to the map and pulled it up. Written on the board underneath was an address in Philadelphia. "Children, as of August first"—she pointed—"I will be here. I am being transferred to St. Patrick's School in Philadelphia."

I heard some moans and several oh no's, but I didn't say anything. After all, my wish had come true. Sister Rose was being transferred! There was no chance of me having her in seventh grade. I was ecstatic, wasn't I?

"I'm going to miss St. Anthony's," she said softly, and her voice broke. "After being here for six years I've made many friends. I hope you'll all copy down my address and write to me. I'd like to know how you're doing."

No way, I told myself. If I did she'd probably send the letter back corrected. But since she was staring straight at me, I pretended to copy the address. I really wrote:

Sister Rose is moving away.
I won't have to worry about
getting her next year.
Hooray!

The bell rang just after Sister gave us our report cards and told us good luck, God bless, and all the stuff the nuns say on the last day of school. But Sister Rose did sound like she meant it, and she looked sad. I felt a tiny bit sad, too, but when the walker bell rang, I stood up, anxious to get out of there and start my vacation.

"Oh, Arlene, could you please stay?" Sister asked.

I groaned inwardly. What could she want with me today? Did she somehow know that I hadn't copied down her address?

Sister said she'd be back shortly. I watched my classmates follow her out into the warm sunshine and freedom.

While I waited, I checked my report card. Wow, was I happy! My Lenten promise had paid off. Sister had given me a B+ in history, a B in geography, and a B in religion. I only got a C in arithmetic, but with my A in English, it was still my best report card ever.

Since Sister still hadn't returned, I roamed the room. There wasn't much to see, so I moved over to the window. Once the kids hit the school yard, they screamed with excitement and scattered like marbles under running feet.

No more pencils, no more books, no more . . . Suddenly I was angry that I was stuck inside. Maybe I'd just leave. School was over. Sister had no right to keep me here.

I noticed her over by the steps talking to Lee. I couldn't tell what they were saying, but before Lee walked away, she patted him on the arm, then turned to come back in.

It was too late to escape so I returned to my desk.

"Oh, Arlene," Sister said, "don't you want to move to one of the front desks?"

I almost said no, but heard myself mutter, "Is this going to take long, Sister?"

"No, I just felt we had some unfinished business to attend to."

My heart skipped a beat.

She sat down and folded those lovely hands together in front of her on the desk.

Now my heart pounded. I didn't like that familiar glint in her eyes.

"I was right and wrong about you, Arlene," she murmured.

I was afraid to ask what that meant.

"You told me a long time ago that I didn't understand you." A slight smile played at the corners of her mouth, but it disappeared so quickly I was certain I'd imagined it.

"When you said that to me, I wanted to . . ." She paused. "I thought you were impudent, but, to be fair, I decided to wait and see."

Why was Sister bringing up something I'd said on the first day of school? Would she also mention what I wrote about her—that she plays favorites?

"Well, Arlene," her voice interrupted my musings, "I'm happy that I reserved my judgment because over the course of this year, I realized I *didn't* understand you—completely. But one thing I do know about you, you speak your mind. That's fine as long as you think it through first. But you don't always do that. Do you?"

I sighed. "No, Sister."

She rose and stood in front of the desk. "I was

taking a big chance giving you Eunice to write about."

The abrupt change of subject surprised me. I guess I must've frowned, because she went on to explain, "I really wanted the class to do those descriptive passages, but I knew it had to be handled carefully. I thought about it and prayed over it a long time before I decided which students should be partners."

"You did?"

She chuckled. "Yes. I knew, for instance, that if I put you and Annette together, you'd probably kill each other."

"How did you . . . ?"

"How did I know you're not exactly buddies? I'm not blind, my dear. I also realized I couldn't let Annette write about Eunice." She glanced out the window, and I was afraid she expected me to say something during the silence. When I didn't, she shook her head and said, "Poor Annette."

I couldn't let *that* pass. "Poor Annette?" I cried.

Sister chuckled. "Many of the things Annette does and says are for attention. And we both know Annette needs an abundance of attention."

Before I had time to think about that, Sister walked to the board and erased her new address, turned, and stared at me again. Why was she always doing that? It made me nervous.

"Eunice tells me you and Nancy Lee have offered to baby-sit for her once a week so she can take an art class at the public school."

155

"Yes, Sister. Eunice's older brother and sister gave her the money for her birthday, but she couldn't go because the class was on a day when they both worked."

"Eunice has been going through a bad time since her mother died," Sister added.

"You knew about that?"

"Of course. That's why I was anxious for her to make some friends. Why I took a chance on you. I knew you were a good writer. But would you handle writing about Eunice in a way that wouldn't hurt or embarrass her? It was a big risk.

"Eunice also told me your aunt has been coming over once in a while to help out with the younger children. Several times she even brought meals."

"My aunt? You mean Aunt Gussie?"

"That's what Eunice said. Your aunt also had a little talk with her about how important appearance is, especially for a young lady. I was glad about that," Sister continued. "I'd tried to broach the subject several times but was afraid it would embarrass her coming from me."

I sat there with my mouth open. "Aunt Gussie never said a word. Neither did Eunice." Why should I be surprised? Aunt Gussie never bragged about the good things she did.

Suddenly Sister Alma stuck her head into the classroom. "Sister, may I speak with you a moment?"

Being alone gave me time to think about everything Sister Rose and I had just discussed. I knew that I'd been wrong about her, at least about some things. She hadn't played favorites. She cared about *all* her students and couldn't treat us the same because we *weren't* the same. She probably never really hated me, though it felt like it at times. I guess what Aunt Gussie had said was true. Sister did all those things to make me a better student.

"I'm sorry to keep you so long," Sister said when she returned. "The main reason I asked you to stay, Arlene, was to congratulate you on winning the English award and to tell you I was proud of the sensitive, caring way you wrote about Eunice. I entered your composition in a creative writing contest the Archdiocese is sponsoring."

Was Sister Rose actually saying she was proud of me?

"The composition was good, Arlene. I have high hopes for it. You should receive a list of the winners sometime during the summer."

I was speechless.

"I enjoy teaching creative writing, and it's gratifying to see talent taking shape."

"Talent?"

"Yes, Arlene, you are talented. But you are also lazy and a procrastinator. That's why I kept hammering at you all year. You'll never be a good writer by putting things off. Try to write something every day."

I nodded.

We were both quiet a moment. Then Sister opened her desk drawer and removed a package wrapped in tissue paper. "This is for you."

I gasped. "Me?"

"Open it."

I could tell it was a book and told myself not to act disappointed if it was one about the saints. My hands shook as I tore away the wrappings. It wasn't a holy book.

She smiled. "Every writer needs a thesaurus. I'm disappointed I won't have you in my class next year. Before I received my transfer from the Mother House, Sister Alma told me I'd be teaching seventh grade next year. I would have liked to see your progress as a writer."

For a minute I was afraid I might cry, but that sure would have been stupid. Wasn't I finally getting everything I wanted?

"Is there something wrong with the book?"

"Oh, no, Sister, it's great. Thank you. I just . . ." How could I tell her what I was feeling when I wasn't sure myself?

Sister glanced at her watch. "I must be going. I'm late for lunch." Holding out her hand, she said, "God keep you in his care."

I stood up and took her hand. She held mine in both of hers. "I expect big things from you, Arlene. Don't disappoint me."

We smiled at each other and those blue eyes stared into mine as they had so many times during the year.

Then, with a swish of her long black skirt, she was gone. I gazed after her until my eyes were drawn to the place on the blackboard where her new address had been. I stared at it a moment before thinking, I hope Nancy Lee copied it down. If not, I could probably get it from Eunice.